Penguin Twentieth-Century Classics
The Master of Go

Yasunari Kawabata, winner of the 1968 N̶   ̶ture,
was born near Osaka in 1899 and was   ̶ or two. As
a boy, he had hoped to become a̶   n̶ still reflected
in his novels. But his first stories   while he was still in
high school and he decided to be̶   ̶iter. He graduated from
Tokyo Imperial University in 192̶   ̶d a year later made his first
impact on Japanese letters with *Izu Dancer*. He soon became a leading
figure in the lyrical school that offered the chief challenge to the
proletarian literature of the late 1920s. His writings combine the two
forms of the novel and the *haiku* poem, which within the restrictions
of a rigid metre achieves a startling beauty by its juxtaposition of
opposite and incongruous terms. *Snow Country* (1956) and *Thousand
Cranes* (1959) made him known in this country. These two books
have been published together in one volume by Penguin (1971).

Kawabata's *House of the Sleeping Beauties*, *The Sound of the Mountain*
(Penguin, 1974) and *Beauty and Sadness* have also appeared in English.
Kawabata was also eminent as a literary critic, and discovered and
sponsored such remarkable writers as Yukio Mishima. Like so many
other Japanese writers, he lived in Kamakura. On 16 April 1972, at
the age of seventy-three, Kawabata died by his own hand.

Yasunari Kawabata

The Master of Go

Translated from the Japanese
by Edward G. Seidensticker

Penguin Books

PENGUIN BOOKS

Published by the Penguin Group
27 Wrights Lane, London w8 5TZ, England
Viking Penguin Inc., 40 West 23rd Street, New York, New York 10010, USA
Penguin Books Australia Ltd, Ringwood, Victoria, Australia
Penguin Books Canada Ltd, 2801 John Street, Markham, Ontario, Canada L3R 1B4
Penguin Books (NZ) Ltd, 182–190 Wairau Road, Auckland 10, New Zealand

Penguin Books Ltd, Registered Offices: Harmondsworth, Middlesex, England

Published in Japanese as Meijin by *Shincho* magazine, Tokyo
Translation published in USA 1972
Published in Great Britain by Martin Secker & Warburg Ltd 1973
Published in Penguin Books 1976
10 9 8 7 6 5 4 3 2 1

Made and printed in Great Britain by
Richard Clay Ltd, Bungay, Suffolk
Typeset in Monotype Bembo

Introduction

Mr Kawabata has described *The Master of Go* as 'a faithful chronicle-novel'. The word used, of course, is not 'novel' but *shōsetsu*, a rather more flexible and generous and catholic term than 'novel'. Frequently what would seem to the Western reader a piece of autobiography or a set of memoirs, somewhat embroidered and coloured but essentially non-fiction all the same, is placed by the Japanese reader in the realm of the *shōsetsu*.

So it is with *The Master of Go*. It contains elements of fiction, but it is rather more chronicle than novel, a sad, elegant piece of reportage, based upon a 1938 Go match, the course of which was precisely as described in this 'chronicle-novel', and upon which Mr Kawabata reported for the twin Osaka and Tokyo newspapers that today both bear the name *Mainichi*.

Certain elements of fiction are obvious. Mr Kawabata gives himself a fictitious name, Uragami, and apparently, though the matter could be a small failure of memory, assigns himself a different age from that which is actually his. The Master is known by his own name, or rather his professional name, but, as if to emphasize that the Master is the protagonist, always at the centre of things, Mr Kawabata also assigns the adversary, in real life Mr Kitani Minoru, a fictitious name. The complex treatment of time, with the action beginning and ending at the same point, and the delicate, impressionistic descriptions of setting and season are further justification for the expression 'chronicle-novel'.

But the most complex element of fiction probably is in the delineation of the Master himself. Persons who knew him in real life have told us that in addition to being almost grotesquely diminutive, he gave an impression of deviousness and even of a certain foxlike slyness. He had, at least to the casual observer, little of the nobility with which Mr Kawabata has endowed him. Mr Kawabata's achievement thus transcends faithful chronicling and becomes fictional characterization of a virtuoso order.

Shūsai the Master becomes a sad and noble symbol. In what is perhaps the most famous of all his pronouncements, Mr Kawabata said shortly after the war that henceforward he would be able to write only elegies. The defeat of 1945 was, along with the loss of all his immediate relatives in childhood, one of the great events moulding the Kawabata sensibility. He began reworking his chronicle of the 1938 Go match during the war, and did not complete it until nearly a decade after the end of the war. The symbolic reality breathed into its central character makes *The Master of Go* the most beautiful of his elegies.

'The invincible Master' lost his final championship match, and at Mr Kawabata's hands the defeat becomes the defeat of a tradition. It is the aristocratic tradition which, until 1945, was the grounding for morals and ethics in Japan, and for the arts as well. Just as Mr Kawabata would have nothing of jingoistic wartime hysteria, so he would have nothing of the platitudinous 'democracy' and 'liberalism' of the post-war years. He was not prepared to turn his back on what was for him the essence of Japan. One was puzzled to know why the flamboyant Mishima Yukio and the quiet, austere Kawabata should have felt so close to each other. Perhaps a part of the secret lies in the aristocratic tendencies the two men shared.

The game of Go is simple in its fundamentals and infinitely complex in the execution of them. It is not what might be called a game of moves, as chess and chequers. Though captured stones may be taken from the board, a stone is never moved to a second position after it has been placed upon one of the three hundred and sixty-one points to which play is confined. The object is to build up positions which are invulnerable to enemy attack, meanwhile surrounding and capturing enemy stones.

A moment's deliberation upon the chart of the completed game should serve to establish that Black controls major territories at the lower left and the upper right of the board, and that White is strong at the lower right. Black controls a lesser area at the upper left and White at the left centre. The upper central regions of the board are delicately divided between the two, and the centre and the regions immediately below are neutral. A very special sort of visual faculty seems required for the final summing up, and, one might say, a sort of kinetic faculty too. Persons who know Go well have been able to give me a reasonably clear account of the 1938 game only by lining the stones up one by one as they were in fact played.

When, in 1954, *The Master of Go* first appeared in book form, it was somewhat longer than the version translated here. The shorter version is Mr Kawabata's own favourite, for it is the one included in the most recent edition of his 'complete works'. The portions excised from the 1954 version fall between the end of the match and the Master's death.

I am very greatly in debt to Miss Ibuki Kazuko and Mr Yanagita Kunio, both of the Chūō Kōron Publishing Company in Tokyo. Out of sheer kindness, they were more help in solving the mysteries of the text and the game than a platoon of paid researchers could have been.

January 1972   E. G. S.

Publisher's Acknowledgement

New diagrams, showing the progress of the match, were prepared for this Penguin edition by Stuart Dowsey, Director of the London Go Centre.

The
Master
of Go

Shūsai, Master of Go, twenty-first in the Honimbō succession, died in Atami, at the Urokoya Inn, on the morning of 18 January 1940. He was sixty-seven years old by the Oriental count.

18 January is an easy day to remember in Atami. 'Remember in years to come the moon of this night of this month,' said Kan'ichi in the famous scene from Kōyō's melodramatic novel of the nineties, *Demon Gold*, the parting on the beach at Atami. The night to be remembered is 17 January, and the Kōyō festival is held in Atami on the anniversary. The Master's death came the following day.

Literary observances always accompany the festival. In 1940 they were elaborate as never before, honouring not only Kōyō himself but two other writers whose bonds with Atami had been strong, Takayama Chogyū and Tsubouchi Shōyō. And three novelists, Takeda Toshihiko, Osaragi Jirō, and Hayashi Fusao, who had during the year treated of Atami in their writings, were presented with testimonials by the city. Being at the time in Atami, I attended the festival.

On the evening of 17 January, the mayor gave a banquet at my inn, the Juraku. I was awakened at dawn by a telephone call informing me of the Master's death. I went immediately to the Urokoya to pay my final respects. After breakfast, back at my inn, I went with writers and city officials to lay flowers at Shōyō's grave, and then to the plum orchard, where, in the Bushōan Pavilion, there was another banquet. Slipping out midway through the banquet, I went again to the Urokoya, took pictures of the dead man, and saw the body off to Tokyo.

The Master had come to Atami on the fifteenth, and on the

eighteenth he was dead. It was as if he had come to Atami to die. I had visited him on the sixteenth and played two games of Shōgi[1] with him. He took a sudden turn for the worse that evening, very shortly after I had left him. Those were his last games of the Shōgi of which he was so fond. I did the newspaper accounts of his last championship match at Go, I was his last adversary at Shōgi, and I was the last to take his picture.

I came to know him well when the *Tokyo Nichinichi Shimbun* (now the *Mainichi Shimbun*) invited me to report on that last match. Even for a match sponsored by a newspaper the ceremonies were elaborate, without equal in the years since. The match began in Tokyo on 26 June 1938, at the Kōyōkan Restaurant in Shiba Park, and ended on 4 December, in Itō, at the Dankōen Inn. A single game took almost half a year. There were fourteen sessions. My report was serialized in sixty-four instalments.[2] There was, to be sure, a three-month recess, from mid-August to mid-November, because the Master fell seriously ill. It was a critical illness that added much to the pathos. One may say that in the end the match took the Master's life. He never quite recovered, and in upwards of a year he was dead.

2

To be quite precise, the match ended at 2.42 on the afternoon of 4 December 1938. The last play was Black 237, by the Master's opponent.

Silently, the Master filled in a neutral point.

'It will be five points?' said one of the judges, Onoda of the Sixth Rank, his manner polite and distant. He probably spoke from solicitude for the Master, whom he wished to spare the discomfort of having the board rearranged on the spot,[3] and his defeat by five points made quite clear.

'Yes, five points,' muttered the Master. Looking up through swollen eyelids, he made no motion towards rearranging the board.

None among the functionaries who crowded the room was able to speak.

'If I hadn't gone into the hospital we would have had it over with at Hakoné.' The Master spoke calmly, as if to relieve the heaviness in the air.

He asked how much time he had used in play.

'White – nineteen hours and fifty-seven minutes. Three minutes more, sir, and it would have been exactly half the time you were allowed,' said the youth who was keeping the records. 'Black used thirty-four hours and nineteen minutes.'

High-ranking players are usually given ten hours of play, but for this match an exception was made and the time allotment increased fourfold. Black still had several hours left, but the thirty-four hours he had used were extraordinary all the same, indeed probably unique in all the annals of the game since the imposition of time limits.

It was almost three when the game ended. The maid came with tea. The company sat in silence, all eyes on the Go board.

The Master poured for his opponent, Otaké of the Seventh Rank.

Since offering the proper words of thanks at the end of the game, the young Otaké had sat motionless, head bowed. His hands rested side by side on his knees, his always pale face was blanched.

Roused by the Master, who had begun to put away the white stones, he began putting the black stones in their bowl. The Master stood up and, as on ordinary days, nonchalantly left the room. He had offered no comment on the play. The younger player of course had no comment to make. Matters might have been different had he been the loser.

Back in my room, I looked out the window. With astonishing speed Otaké had changed to a padded kimono and stepped down into the garden. He was sitting on a bench at the far side, all alone, arms tightly folded. His eyes were on the ground. His attitude there in the wide, cold garden, in the approaching twilight of late autumn, suggested deep meditation.

I opened a glass door at the veranda. 'Mr Otaké,' I called. 'Mr Otaké.'

He turned and glanced up at me, as if in annoyance. Perhaps he was weeping.

I went back into my room. The Master's wife had come in. 'It has been a long time, and you have been very good to us.'

I exchanged a few remarks with her, and Otaké had already left the garden. With another quick change, he made the rounds, this time in formal kimono, of the Master's room and the rooms of the various managers and organizers. He came to my room as well.

I went to pay my respects to the Master.

3

A day after the end of that half-year contest, the managers and the rest were in a rush to be off. It was the day before the test run on the new Itō railway line.

With trains coming through just at the holiday season, the main street was bright with festive decorations. I had been in seclusion at the inn, 'sealed in a tin can', as the process of keeping the game shut off from the world is described. Now, on the bus for home, the decorations bright around me, I felt liberated, as if I had emerged from a dark cave. The raw earth of the roads around the new station, the flimsy houses – the jumble and disorder of the new town spoke to me of all the vital world outside.

As the bus left Itō and set out along the coast road, we passed women with bundles of brushwood on their backs. Some carried white-leafed ferns, decorations for the New Year, in their hands, some had ferns tied to their brushwood. I suddenly wanted to be among people. It was as if I had come over a mountain and caught sight of smoke from a village beyond. I longed for the routines of ordinary life, preparations for the New Year and the like. I felt as if I had fled some morbid, distorted world. The women had gathered their firewood and were on their way home for dinner. The sea shone with a light so dull that one could not guess its source. The colour, at the edge of darkness, was of winter.

Even on the bus I thought of the Master. Perhaps my longing for company had to do with my feelings for him.

The last of the people in attendance on the game had withdrawn, and only the aged Master and his wife were left at the Itō inn.

'The invincible Master' had lost his last championship match. One would have thought he would be the first to wish to leave; and to recover from the strain of having fought both Otaké and illness, the best thing, one would have thought, would have been an immediate change of air. Was the Master perhaps somewhat vague in these matters? Though all the various organizers, and myself as well, reporter on the game, had come to find the place intolerable and had left as if seeking refuge, the defeated Master stayed behind alone. Would he be sitting there absently as always, leaving the gloom and the weariness to the imagination of others, as if to say that he knew nothing about them?

His opponent, Otaké of the Seventh Rank, had been among the first to go. Unlike the childless Master, he had a lively house to go back to.

I believe it was two or three years after the match that I had a letter from his wife in which she said that they now had sixteen people in the house. I wanted to pay a visit. I did call with condolences after his father died and that total of sixteen had been reduced to fifteen. The visit, my first, was rather belated, for it came a full month, I believe, after the funeral. Otaké himself was out, but his wife showed me into the parlour. Her manner suggested that I brought pleasant memories. When we had finished our greetings she stepped to the door.

'Have them all come in, please.'

There was a rush of footsteps and four or five young people came into the parlour. They formed a row, like children being called to attention. Apparently disciples of Otaké's, they ranged from perhaps eleven or twelve to twenty. Among them was a tall, plump, red-cheeked girl.

'Now be polite,' said Mrs Otaké, having introduced me.

They bobbed their heads abruptly. I felt the warmth of the household. There was nothing calculated about the scene, the house was one in which such things came quite naturally. When the young people had left the parlour I could hear them chattering noisily through the house. Mrs Otaké invited me upstairs, where I had a practice game with one of them. She brought in dish after dish, and in the end my visit was a long one.

That household of sixteen persons included disciples. Among the younger professional players, no one else kept four or five disciples in his house. In that fact was evidence of Otaké's popularity and affluence, of course, but perhaps his strongly domestic inclinations and his great attachment to his own children reached out to embrace these others.

'Sealed in a tin can' during that last match, Otaké would call his wife immediately at the end of a session.

'Today the Master was good enough to play until . . . ,' and he would give her the number of the last play.

He reported only so much, offering nothing that might hint at the progress of the match. I would hear him make his report and think how much I liked him.

4

On the day of the opening ceremony at the Kōyōkan, Black made a single play and White a single play; and the next day took them only up to White 12. The match was then moved to Hakoné. The Master and the various managers and attendants set out together. Real play not having begun, signs of discord still lay in the future. On the evening of our arrival at the Taiseikan in Dōgashima, the Master relaxed with his usual aperitif, something less than a flagon of saké, and talked of this and that with richly expressive gestures; and so the evening passed.

The large table in the parlour to which we had first been shown seemed to be of Tsugaru lacquer. The talk turned to lacquer, of which the Master had this to say:

'I don't remember when it was, but I once saw a Go board of lacquer. It wasn't just lacquer-coated, it was dry lacquer to the core. A lacquer man in Aomori made it for his own amusement. He took twenty-five years to do it, he said. I imagine it *would* take that long, waiting for the lacquer to dry and then putting on a new coat. The bowls and boxes were solid lacquer too. He showed the set at an exhibition and asked five thousand, and when it didn't sell he came to the Go Association and asked them to sell it for three thousand. But I don't know. It was too heavy. Heavier than I am. It must have weighed close to a hundred and twenty pounds.' And, looking at Otaké: 'You've put on weight.'

'Over a hundred and thirty.'

'Oh? Exactly twice what I am. And you're less than half my age.'

'I've turned thirty, sir. Thirty is a bad age. In the days when you were good enough to give me lessons I was thinner.' His thoughts turned to his boyhood. 'I was sick a great deal in those days. Your lady was very kind to me.'

From talk of the hot springs of Shinshū, Mrs Otaké's home, the conversation moved to domestic matters. Otaké had married at twenty-three, when he had reached the Fifth Rank. He had three children and kept three disciples in his house, which thus contained ten persons.

His oldest, a girl of six, had learned the game from watching him.

'I gave her a nine-stone handicap the other day. I've kept a chart of the game.'

'Very remarkable,' the Master too had to admit.

'And my second, the four-year-old, knows all about putting stones in check. I suppose we can't tell yet whether they have talent, but there might be possibilities.'

The others seemed uncomfortable.

Apparently Otaké, one of the eminences of the Go world, was thinking seriously that if his two daughters, six and four, showed promise, he would make them professionals like himself. It is said that talent in Go appears at about ten, and that if a child does not begin his studies by that age there is no hope for him. Yet Otaké's words struck me as odd. Did they tell, perhaps, of youth, of a thirty-year-old who was a captive of Go but had not yet been bled by it? His household must be a happy one, I thought.

The Master spoke of his own house. It stood on something under a quarter of an acre in Setagaya, but since the house itself covered almost a third of the land, the garden was somewhat cramped. He would like to sell and move to a house with even slightly more spacious grounds. For the Master, family meant himself and his wife, who was here beside him. He no longer kept disciples in his house.

5

When the Master was released from St Luke's, the match, recessed for three months, was resumed at the Dankōen in Itō. On the first day there were only five plays, from Black 101 to Black 105. A dispute arose over scheduling the next session. Otaké rejected the modified rules the Master proposed for reasons of health, and said that he would forfeit the game. The dispute was more stubbornly complicated than a similar disagreement had been at Hakoné.

Tense days followed one another as the contestants and managers remained 'sealed in' at the Dankōen. One day the Master drove to Kawana for a change of air. It was most remarkable for a man who hated such excursions to venture forth on his own. I went with him, as did Murashima of the Fifth Rank, who was one of his disciples, and the young girl, herself a professional Go player, who was keeping the records.

But it seemed wrong that, having arrived at the Kawana Hotel, the Master had nothing to do except sit in the vast Western-style lounge and drink orange pekoe.

Glass-enclosed, the semicircular lounge thrust forward into the garden. It was like an observatory or a sun room. To the left and right of the broad lawn were golf courses, the Fuji course and the Oshima course. Beyond the lawn and the golf courses was the sea.

I had long been fond of the bright, open view from Kawana. I had thought I would show it to the gloomy old man, and I watched to see his reaction. He sat in silence, as if not even aware of the view before him. He did not look at the other guests. There was no change in his expression and he had nothing to say about the scenery or about the hotel; and so, as always, his wife was his spokesman and prompter. She praised the scene and invited him to agree. He neither nodded assent nor offered objection.

Wanting him to be in the bright sunlight, I invited him into the garden.

'Yes, do let's go out,' said his wife. 'You won't have to worry about getting a chill, and it's sure to make you feel better.'

She was helping me. The Master did not seem to find the request an imposition.

It was one of those warm late-autumn days when the island of Oshima lies in a mist. Kites skimmed and dipped over the warm, calm sea. At the far edge of the lawn was a row of pines, framing the sea in green. Several pairs of newly-weds were standing along the line between the grass and the sea. Perhaps because of the brightness and expansiveness of the scene, they seemed unusually self-possessed for newly-weds. From afar, against the pines and the sea, the kimonos seemed fresher and brighter, I thought, than they would have from near at hand. People who came to Kawana belonged to the affluent classes.

'Newly-weds, all of them, I suppose,' I said to the Master, feeling an envy that approached resentment.

'They must be bored,' he muttered.

Long after, I remembered the expressionless voice.

I would have liked to stroll on the lawn, to sit on it; but the Master stood fixed to one spot, and I could only stand there beside him.

We had the car return by way of Lake Ippeki. The little lake was surprisingly beautiful, deep and quiet in the afternoon sun of late autumn. The Master too got out and briefly gazed at it.

Pleased with the brightness of the Kawana Hotel, I took Otaké there the next morning. I was being fatherly. I hoped the place might do a little towards untying the emotional knots. I invited Yawata, the secretary of the Go Association, and Sunada of the *Nichinichi Shimbun* to go with us. For lunch we had sukiyaki in a rustic cottage on the hotel grounds. We stayed until evening. I was well acquainted with the place, having gone there by myself and with a group of dancers as well as at the invitation of Okura Kishichirō, the founder of the Okura enterprises. The dispute continued after our return from Kawana. Even bystanders like myself felt constrained to mediate. The match was finally resumed on 25 November.

The Master had a large oval brazier of paulownia beside him and an oblong brazier behind him, on which he kept water boiling. At the urging of Otaké, he wrapped himself in a muffler, and as further protection against the cold he had on a sort of over-cloak, which seemed to be of blanket cloth with a knitted lining. In his room he was never without it. He had a slight fever this morning, he said.

'And what is your normal temperature, sir?' asked Otaké as he sat down at the board.

'It runs between ninety-six and ninety-seven,' said the Master quietly, as if savouring the words. 'It never goes as high as ninety-seven.'

On another occasion, asked his height, he said: 'I was just under five feet when I had my draft examination. Then I grew a half inch and was over five feet. You lose height as you get older, and now it's exactly five feet.'

'He has a body like an undernourished child,' said the doctor when the Master fell ill at Hakoné. 'There's no flesh at all on his calves. You wonder how he manages to carry himself. I can't prescribe medicine in ordinary doses. I have to give him what a thirteen- or fourteen-year-old might take.'

6

That the Master seemed to grow larger when he seated himself before the Go board had to do of course with the power and prestige of his art, the rewards of long training and discipline; but his trunk was disproportionately long. He also had a large, longish face, on which the individual features were bold. The strong jaw was especially conspicuous. These various characteristics were apparent in the pictures I took of the dead face.

I was most apprehensive through the days when they were being developed. I always had my developing and printing done at the Nonomiya studio in Kudan. When I delivered the film I described the circumstances, and asked that the film be treated with particular care.

After the Kōyō Festival I returned home for a time and then went again to Atami. I gave my wife strict instructions that if the pictures of the dead face were received in Kamakura she was to send them immediately to the Juraku in Atami, and that she was neither to look at them herself nor to let anyone else see them. I thought that if my amateur photographs showed the Master to disadvantage I would not wish to do injury to his memory by having people see them or even hear of them. I thought that if they turned out badly I would burn them without showing them to the Master's widow or disciples. It was not at all unlikely that I had failed, since the shutter of my camera was defective.

I had come at a telephone summons from my wife when, with other participants in the Kōyō Festival, I was having a lunch of turkey sukiyaki in the plum orchard. She told me that the widow wanted me to take pictures of the dead man. After my visit that morning, it had occurred to me that, if the widow wanted photographs or a death mask, I myself might take responsibility for the former, and I had told my wife, who called later with condolences, to pass the message on. The widow had replied that she did not want a death mask, but would appreciate photographs.

But when the time came I quite lost confidence. It was a heavy duty I had taken upon myself. And the shutter of my camera had a way of catching, and the chances of failure seemed great. Remembering that a photographer had been brought from Tokyo to cover the festival, I asked him to photograph the dead Master. The widow and the others might object if I were suddenly to introduce a photographer who had been nothing to the Master, but it was certain that the pictures would be better than any I myself might take. Objections came instead from the organizers of the festival: they had brought the man for the festival, and it would be a great inconvenience to have him dispatched elsewhere. They were of course right. My feelings about the Master had been mine alone, and I was unconsciously at odds with the other participants in the festival. I asked the photographer to look at my camera. He said that I should open it to voluntary timing and use my hand as a shutter. He changed the film for me. I went to the Urokoya in a cab.

The night doors were closed in the room where the Master had been laid, and the light was on. The widow and her younger brother went in with me.

'Is it too dark?' asked the brother. 'Shall we open the doors?'

I took perhaps ten pictures. I was careful that the shutter did not catch, and I tried the technique of using my hand as a shutter. I would have liked to take pictures from all sides and angles, but out of respect for the dead man I could not bring myself to wander through the room. I took all my pictures from a single kneeling position.

Presently they came from my house in Kamakura. My wife

had written on the back of the envelope: 'These have just come from the Nonomiya. I have not opened them. You are to be at the shrine office by five on the fourth.' The last message had to do with the spring rites at the Hachiman Shrine in Kamakura. Kamakura writers born under the sign of the zodiac under which this year fell were to perform the exorcism.[4]

I opened the envelope, and immediately was the captive of the dead face. The pictures were a success. They were of a man asleep, and at the same time they had the quiet of death about them.

I had knelt at the side of the dead Master, who lay on his back, and so I was looking up at him from an angle. The absence of a pillow was the mark of death, and the face was tilted ever so slightly upward, so the strong jaw and the large mouth, just perceptibly open, stood out even more prominently. The powerful nose seemed almost oppressively large. There was profound sorrow in the wrinkles at the closed eyes and the heavily shaded forehead.

The light through the half-opened night doors came from the feet, and the light from the ceiling struck the lower part of the face; and, since the head tilted slightly backward, the forehead was in shadow. The light struck from the jaw over the cheeks, and thence towards the rise of the eyebrows and hollow eyes to the bridge of the nose. Looking more closely, I saw that the lower lip was in shadow and the upper lighted, and between them, in the deep shadow of the mouth, a single upper tooth could be seen. White hairs stood out in the short moustache. There were two large moles on the right cheek, the farther from the camera. I had caught their shadows, and the shadows too of the veins at the temples and forehead. Horizontal wrinkles crossed the forehead. Only a single tuft of the short-cropped hair above caught the light. The Master had stiff, coarse hair.

7

The two large moles were on the right cheek, and the right eyebrow was extraordinarily long. The far end drew an arc over the eyelid, and reached even to the line of the closed eye. Why should the camera have made it seem so long? The eyebrow and the two moles seemed to add a gently pleasing melancholy to the dead face.

The long eyebrow brought twinges of sorrow. This was the reason.

When my wife and I visited the Urokoya on 16 January, two days before the Master's death, his wife said: 'Yes. We were going to mention it as soon as these good people came. Do you remember? We were going to mention your eyebrow.' She cast a prompting glance at the Master, then turned to us. 'I am sure it was on the twelfth. Rather a warm day, I believe. We thought it would be right for the trip to Atami if he were to have a good shave, and so we called a barber we've known for years. My husband went out into the sunlight on the veranda for his shave. He seemed to remember something. He said to the barber that he had one very long hair in his left eyebrow. It was a sign of long life, he said, and the barber was not to touch it. The barber stopped work and said yes, there it was, this one right here. A hair of good luck, a sign of long life. He would indeed be careful. My husband turned to me and said that Mr Uragami had written about the hair in his newspaper articles. Mr Uragami had a remarkable eye for details, he said. He had not noticed it himself until he read about it in the paper. He was overcome with admiration.'

Though the Master was silent as always, a flicker crossed his face as if it had caught the shadow of a passing bird. I was uncomfortable.

But I did not dream that the Master would be dead two days after the story of the mark of longevity he had asked the barber to spare.

It was a trifling matter, that I should have noticed the hair and written about it; but I had noticed it at a difficult moment, and it had come as a sort of rescue. I had written thus of the day's session at Hakoné:[5]

The Master's wife is staying at the inn, ministering to her aged husband. Mrs Otaké, mother of three children, the oldest of them six, commutes between Hiratsuka and Hakoné. The strain on the two wives is painfully apparent to the onlooker. On 10 August, for instance, during the play at Hakoné, when the Master was desperately ill, the faces of the two women seemed drained of blood, their expressions were tense and drawn.

The Master's wife had not been at the Master's side during play; but today she sat gazing intently from the next room. She was not watching the play. She was watching the ailing player, and she did not take her eyes from him all through the session.

Mrs Otaké has never come into the room during play. Today she was in the hall, now standing still, now walking up and down. Finally, the suspense too much for her, it seemed, she went into the managers' office.

'Otaké is still thinking about his next play?'

'Yes. It's a difficult moment.'

'It's never easy to concentrate, but it would be easier if he had slept last night.'

Otaké had worried the whole night through about whether to continue the game with the ailing Master. He had not slept at all, and had come sleepless to the session that morning. It was Black's turn at half past twelve, the hour specified for breaking off the session, and after almost an hour and a half Otaké still had not decided upon his sealed play. There was no question of lunch. Mrs Otaké of course found it difficult to sit quietly in her room. She too had passed a sleepless night.

The only one who slept was Mr Otaké, Junior. He is a splendid young man now in his eighth month, so splendid that if someone were to inquire of me about the nature and the spirit of Mr Otaké,

Senior, I would want to show him the child, a veritable embodiment of that spirit. It has been one of those days when a person finds it impossible to face an adult, and for me this little Momotarō has been a saviour.

Today I discovered for the first time a white hair about an inch long in the Master's eyebrow. Standing out from the swollen-eyed, heavy-veined face, it too somehow came as a saviour.

From the veranda outside the players' room, which was ruled by a sort of diabolic tension, I glanced out into the garden, beaten down by the powerful summer sun, and saw a girl of the modern sort insouciantly feeding the carp. I felt as if I were looking at some freak. I could scarcely believe that we belonged to the same world.

The faces of both the Master's wife and Mrs Otaké were drawn and pale and wasted. As always, the Master's wife left the room when play began, but almost immediately she was back again, and she sat gazing at the Master from the next room. Onoda of the Sixth Rank was there too, his eyes closed and his head bowed. The face of the writer Muramatsu Shōfū, who had been among the observers, wore a pitying expression. Even the talkative Otaké was silent. He seemed unable to look up at the Master's face.

The sealed play, White 90, was opened. Inclining his head to the left and to the right, the Master played White 92, cutting the diagonal black stones. White 94 was played after a long period of meditation, an hour and nine minutes. Now closing his eyes, now looking aside, occasionally bowing as if to control a spell of nausea, the Master seemed in great distress. His figure was without the usual grandeur. Perhaps because I was watching against the light, the outlines of his face seemed blurred, ghostlike. The room was quiet, but with a different quietness. The stones striking the board – Black 95, White 96, Black 97 – had an unearthly quality about them, as of echoing in a chasm.

The Master deliberated for more than half an hour before playing White 98. His eyes blinking, his mouth slightly open, he fanned himself as if fanning up the embers in the deepest reaches of his being. Was such grim concentration necessary, I wondered.

Yasunaga of the Fourth Rank came in. Just inside the room, he knelt down to make his formal greetings. His bow was solemnly respectful and diffident. Neither contestant noticed. Each time one or the other seemed about to look his way, Yasunaga repeated the bow. There was nothing else for him to do. Demonic forces seemed lost in horrid battle.

Immediately after White 98 the youth who was keeping records announced that a minute of play remained. Then it was twelve thirty, time for the sealed play.

'If you are tired, sir,' said Onoda to the Master, 'suppose you leave.'

'Yes, do, please, sir, if you feel like it,' said Otaké, back from the lavatory. 'I'll think for a while by myself here, and seal my play. I promise not to ask for advice.' For the first time there was laughter.

They spoke out of concern for the Master, whom it seemed inhuman to keep longer at the board. There was no real need for him to be there, since Otaké's Black 99 would be a sealed play. His head cocked to one side, the Master deliberated whether to stay or to go.

'I'll stay just a little longer.' But immediately he went to the lavatory, and then he was joking with Muramatsu Shōfū in the anteroom. He was surprisingly lively when away from the board.

Left to himself, Otaké gazed at the White pattern in the lower left corner as if he wanted to sink his fangs into it. An hour and thirteen minutes later, at well past one, he made his sealed play, Black 99, a 'peep'⁶ at the dead centre of the board.

In the morning the managers had gone to ask the Master whether he wanted to play in an outbuilding or on the second floor of the main building.

'I can't walk any more,' was his answer, 'and I'd prefer the main building. But Mr Otaké said the waterfall bothered him. Suppose you ask him. I'll do as he wishes.'

8

I had written of the long white hair in the left eyebrow. In my pictures of the dead face, however, the right eyebrow was the thicker. It hardly seemed likely that the right eyebrow had suddenly begun to grow after his death. And had he really had such long eyebrows? One might have concluded that the camera was exaggerating, but probably it had told the truth.

I need not have been so apprehensive. My Contax had a Sonner 1.5 lens. It had performed quite on its own, without promptings from me. For a lens there was neither living nor dead, there was neither man nor object, not sentimentality or reverence. I had made no great mistake with my Sonner 1.5, and that, I suppose, was that. The face was dead, and the richness and softness were perhaps the work of the lens.

I was struck by a certain intensity of feeling in the pictures. Was it in the dead face itself? The face was rich in feeling, yet the dead man himself had none. It seemed to me that the pictures were neither of life nor of death. The face was alive but sleeping. One might in another sense see them as pictures of a dead face and yet feel in them something neither living nor dead. Was it that the face came through as the living face? Was it that the face called up so many memories of the living man? Or was it that I had before me not the living face but photographs? I thought it strange too that in pictures I could see the dead face more clearly and minutely than when I had had it before me. The pictures were like a symbol of something hidden, something that must not be looked upon.

Afterwards I regretted having taken the pictures. It had been heedless of me. Dead faces should not leave behind photographs. Yet it was a fact that the Master's remarkable life came to me in the pictures.

No one could have described the Master's face as handsome or noble. It was indeed a common sort of face, with no single feature of great merit. The ears, for instance – the lobes were as if they had been smashed. The mouth was large, the eyes were small. Through long years of discipline in his art, the Master seated at the Go board had the power to quiet his surroundings, and that same force of spirit was in my pictures too. There was a deep sadness in the lines of the closed eyelids, as of one grieving in sleep.

And I looked at the body. The head of a doll, and the head only, seemed to protrude from the honeycomb pattern of the rough-woven kimono. Because the body had been dressed in an Oshima kimono after the Master's death, there was a bunching at the shoulders. Yet one had from it the feeling one had of the Master in life, as if from the waist he dwindled away to nothing. The Master's legs and hips: as the doctor had said at Hakoné, they seemed scarcely enough to bear his weight. Taken from the Urokoya, the body had seemed quite weightless save for the head. During that last match I had noticed the thinness of the seated Master's knees and in my pictures too there seemed to be only a head, almost gruesome, somehow, as if severed. There was something unreal about the pictures, which may have come from the face, the ultimate in tragedy, of a man so disciplined in an art that he had lost the better part of reality. Perhaps I had photographed the face of a man meant from the outset for martyrdom to art. It was as if the life of Shūsai, Master of Go, had ended as his art had ended, with that last match.

9

I doubt that there were precedents for the ceremonies that opened the Master's last game. Black made a single play and White a single play, followed by a banquet.

On 26 June 1938, there was a lull in the early-summer rains, and bland summer clouds were in the sky. The foliage in the garden of the Kōyōkan had been washed clean by the rains. Strong sunlight shimmered on a scattering of bamboo leaves.

Seated before the alcove in the downstairs parlour were Honimbō Shūsai, Master of Go, and his challenger, Otaké of the Seventh Rank. All told, four masters were in the assembly:

on Shūsai's left, Sekiné, thirteenth in the line of Grand Masters of Shōgi, as well as Kimura, Master of Shōgi, and Takagi, Master of Renju,[7] all brought together for this the commencement of the Master's last match by the sponsoring newspaper. I myself, special reporter for the newspaper, was beside Takagi. To the right of Otaké were the editor and directors of the newspaper, the secretary and directors of the Japan Go Association, three venerable Go champions of the Seventh Rank, Onoda of the Sixth Rank, who was one of the judges, and various disciples of the Master.

Looking over the assembly, all in formal Japanese dress, the editor made some preliminary remarks. Suspense gripped the room as the Go board was readied at the centre. The Master's little idiosyncrasies as he faced the Go board were once more apparent, especially in the droop of the right shoulder. And the thinness of those knees! The fan seemed huge. Eyes closed, Otaké nodded and inclined his head from side to side.

The Master got up. A folded fan in his hand, he suggested a warrior readying his dirk. He seated himself at the board. The fingers of his left hand in the overskirt of his kimono, his right hand lightly clenched, he raised his head and looked straight before him. Otaké seated himself opposite. After bowing to the Master he took the bowl of black stones from the board and placed them at his right. He bowed again and, motionless, closed his eyes.

'Suppose we begin,' said the Master.

His voice was low but intense, as if he were telling Otaké to be quick about it. Was he objecting to the somewhat histrionic quality of Otaké's behaviour, was he eager to do battle? Otaké opened his eyes and closed them again. During the sessions at Itō he read the *Lotus Sutra* on mornings of play, and he now seemed to be bringing himself to order through silent meditation. Then, quickly, there came a rap of stone on board. It was twenty minutes before noon.

Would it be a new opening or an old, a *hoshi* or a *komoku*?[8]

The world was asking whether Otaké would mount a new offensive or an old. Otaké's play was conservative, at R-16, in the upper right-hand corner; and so one of the mysteries was solved.

His hands on his knees, the Master gazed at the opening *komoku*. Under the gaudy camera lights his mouth was so tightly closed that his lips protruded, and the rest of us seemed to have left his world. This was the third match I had seen the Master play; and always, when he sat before the Go board, he seemed to exude a quiet fragrance that cooled and cleaned the air around him.

After five minutes he seemed about to play, having forgotten that his play was to be sealed.

'I believe we have arranged, sir, that your play should be a sealed one,' said Otaké. 'But I suppose you don't feel that you have played at all unless you have played on the board.'

The Master was led to the next room by the secretary of the Go Association. Closing the door, he noted down his opening play, White 2, on the chart, which he put in an envelope. A sealed play is invalid if anyone besides the player himself sees it.

'We don't seem to have any water,' he said, back at the board. Wetting two fingers with his tongue, he sealed the envelope and signed his name across the seal. Otaké signed below. The envelope was put in a larger envelope, to which one of the managers affixed his seal, and which was then locked in the safe of the Kōyōkan.

The opening ceremonies were over.

Wishing to have pictures taken with which to introduce the match abroad, Kimura Ihei had the players go back to their places. The assembly relaxed, and the venerable gentlemen of the Seventh Rank gathered to admire the board and the stones. There were many estimates as to the thickness of the white stones, perhaps a quarter of an inch, perhaps a fifth.

'They are the best you will find anywhere,' said Kimura,

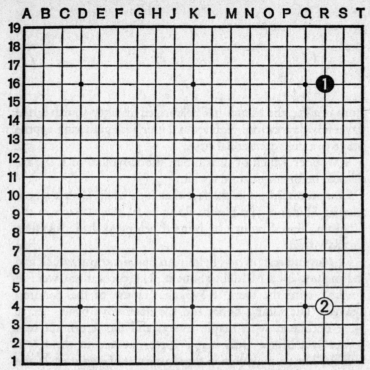

Figure 1: Opening Session (Moves 1 and 2)

Master of Shōgi. 'Perhaps I might be allowed to touch one or two.' He took up a handful.

Go boards can be of great value, and several players had brought boards of which they were proud, as if asking permission to make at least one play in this grandest of matches.

The banquet began after a recess.

Kimura, Master of Shōgi, was thirty-four, Sekiné, thirteenth Grand Master of Shōgi, was seventy-one, and Takagi, Master of Renju, was fifty-one, all by the Oriental count.

Born in 1874, the Master had celebrated his sixty-fourth birth-day a few days before with a modest private gathering appro-priate to a time of national crisis.

'I wonder which of us is older, the Kōyōkan or I,' he re-marked before the second session.

He reminisced upon the fact that such Meiji Go players as Murasé Shūho of the Eighth Rank and Shūei, Master in the Honimbō line to which he himself belonged, had played in this Kōyōkan.

The second session was held in an upstairs room which had the mellow look of Meiji about it. The decorations were in keeping with the name Kōyōkan, 'House of the Autumn Leaves'. The sliding doors and the openwork panels above were decorated with maple leaves, and the screen off in a corner was bright with maple leaves painted in the Kōrin fashion. The arrangement in the alcove was of evergreen leaves and dahlias. The doors of this eighteen-mat room had been opened to the fifteen-mat room next door, so that the some-what exaggerated arrangement did not seem out of place. The dahlias were slightly wilted. No one entered or left the room save a maid with flowered bodkins in a childlike Japanese coif-fure who occasionally came to pour tea. The Master's fan, reflected in a black lacquer tray on which she had brought ice water, was utterly quiet. I was the only reporter present.

Otaké of the Seventh Rank was wearing an unlined black kimono of glossy *habutaé* silk and a crested gossamer-net cloak. Somewhat less formal today, the Master wore a cloak with embroidered crests. The first day's board had been replaced.

The two opening plays had been ceremonial, and serious

play began today. As he deliberated Black 3, Otaké fanned himself and folded his hands behind him, and put the fan on his knee like an added support for the hand on which he now rested his chin. And as he deliberated – see – the Master's breathing was quicker, his shoulders were heaving. Yet there was nothing to suggest disorder. The waves that passed through his shoulders were quite regular. They were to me like a concentration of violence, or the doings of some mysterious power that had taken possession of the Master. The effect was the stronger for the fact that the Master himself seemed unaware of what was happening. Immediately the violence passed. The Master was quiet again. His breathing was normal, though one could not have said at what moment the quiet had come. I wondered if this marked the point of departure, the crossing of the line, for the spirit facing battle. I wondered if I was witness to the workings of the Master's soul as, all unconsciously, it received its inspiration, was host to the afflatus. Or was I watching a passage to enlightenment as the soul threw off all sense of identity and the fires of combat were quenched? Was it what had made 'the invincible Master'?

At the beginning of the session Otaké had offered formal greetings, after which he had said: 'I hope you won't mind, sir, if I have to get up from time to time.'

'I have the same trouble myself,' said the Master. 'I have to get up two and three times every night.'

It was odd that, despite this apparent understanding, the Master seemed to sense none of the nervous tension in Otaké.

When I am at work myself, I drink tea incessantly and am forever having to leave my desk, and sometimes I have nervous indigestion as well. Otaké's trouble was more extreme. He was unique among competitors at the grand spring and autumn tournaments. He would drink enormously from the large pot he kept at his side. Wu[9] of the Sixth Rank, who was at the time one of his more interesting adversaries, also suffered

35

at the Go board from nervous enuresis. I have seen him get up ten times and more in the course of four or five hours of play. Though he did not have Otaké's addiction to tea, there would all the same (and one marvelled at the fact) come sounds from the urinal each time he left the board. With Otaké the difficulty did not stop at enuresis. One noted with curiosity that he would leave his overskirt behind him in the hallway and his obi as well.

After six minutes of thought he played Black 3; and immediately he said, 'Excuse me, please,' and got up. He got up again when he had played Black 5.

The Master had quietly lighted a cigarette from the package in his kimono sleeve.

While deliberating Black 5, Otaké put his hands inside his kimono, and folded his arms, and brought his hands down beside his knees, and brushed an invisible speck of dust from the board, and turned one of the Master's white stones right side up. If the white stones had face and obverse, then the face must be the inner, stripeless side of the clamshell; but few paid attention to such details. The Master would indifferently play his stones with either side up, and Otaké would now and again turn one over.

'The Master is so quiet,' Otaké once said, half jokingly. 'The quiet is always tripping me up. I prefer noise. All this quietness wears me down.'

Otaké was much given to jesting when he was at the board; but since the Master offered no sign that he even noticed, the effect was somewhat blunted. In a match with the Master, Otaké was unwontedly meek.

Perhaps the dignity with which the real professional faces the board comes with middle age, perhaps the young have no use for it. In any case, younger players indulge all manner of odd quirks. To me the strangest was a young player of the Fourth Rank who, at the grand tournament, would open a literary magazine on his knee and read a story while waiting for his adversary to play. When the play had been made, he would look up, deliberate his own play, and, having played, turn nonchalantly to the magazine again. He seemed to be deriding his adversary, and one would not have been surprised had the latter taken umbrage. I heard one day that the young player had shortly afterwards gone insane. Perhaps, given the precarious state of his nerves, he could not tolerate those periods of deliberation.

I have heard that Otaké of the Seventh Rank and Wu of the Sixth once went to a clairvoyant and asked for advice on how to win. The proper method, said the man, was to lose all awareness of self while awaiting an adversary's play. Some years after this retirement match, and shortly before his own death, Onoda of the Sixth Rank, one of the judges at the retirement match, had a perfect record at the grand tournament and gave evidence of remarkable resources left over. His manner at play was equally remarkable. While awaiting a play he would sit quietly with his eyes closed. He explained that he was ridding himself of the desire to win. Shortly after the tournament he went into a hospital, and he died without knowing that he had had stomach cancer. Kubomatsu of the Sixth Rank, who had been one of Otaké's boyhood teachers, also put together an unusual string of victories in the last tournament before his death.

Seated at the board, the Master and Otaké presented a complete contrast, quiet against constant motion, nervelessness against nervous tension. Once he had sunk himself into a session, the Master did not leave the board. A player can often read a great deal into his adversary's manner and expression; but it is said that among professional players the Master alone could read nothing. Yet for all the outward tension, Otaké's game was far from nervous. It was a powerful, concentrated game. Given to long deliberation, he habitually ran out of time. As the deadline approached he would ask the recorder to read off the seconds, and in the final minutes make a hundred plays or a hundred and fifty plays, with a surging violence such as to unnerve his opponent.

Otaké's way of sitting down and getting up again was as if readying himself for battle. It was probably for him what the quickened breathing was for the Master. Yet the heaving of those thin, haunched shoulders was what struck me most forcefully. I felt as if I were the uninvited witness to the secret advent of inspiration, painless, calm, unknown to the Master and not perceived by others.

But afterwards it seemed to me that I had rather outdone myself. Perhaps the Master had but felt a twinge of pain in his chest. His heart condition was worse as the match progressed,

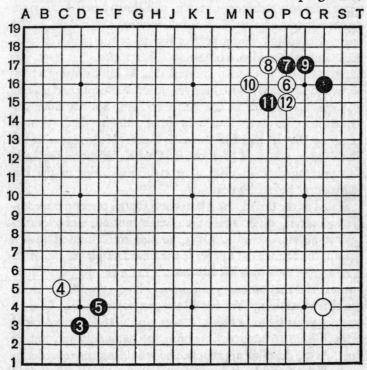

Figure 2: Second Session (Moves 3–12)

and perhaps he had felt the first spasm at that moment. Not knowing of the heart ailment, I had reacted as I had, probably, out of respect for the Master. I should have been more coolly rational. But the Master himself seemed unaware of his illness and of the heavy breathing. No sign of pain or disquiet came over his face, nor did he press a hand to his chest.

Otaké's Black 5 took twenty minutes, and the Master used forty-one minutes for White 6, the first considerable period of deliberation in the match. Since it had been arranged that the player whose turn came at four in the afternoon would seal his play, the sealed play would be the Master's unless he played within two minutes. Otaké's Black 11 had come at two minutes before the hour. The Master sealed his White 12 at twenty-two minutes after the hour.

The skies, clear in the morning, had clouded over. The storm that was to bring floods in both the east and the west of Japan was on its way.[10]

11

The second session at the Kōyōkan was to have begun at ten. Because of a misunderstanding it was delayed until two. I was an onlooker, outside it all; but the consternation of the managers was quite apparent. Virtually the whole of the Association had rushed to the scene, I gathered, and was meeting in another room.

I had arrived just as Otaké was arriving, a large suitcase in his hand.

'Why the luggage?' I asked.

'Yes,' he replied, in the abrupt manner that was his before a session. 'We leave for Hakoné today. To be sealed in for the rest of the match.'

I had been told that the contestants would go directly from the Kōyōkan to a Hakoné inn. Yet the proportions of Otaké's baggage rather startled me.

The Master had made no arrangements for the move.

'Oh was *that* the idea?' he said. 'In that case I should call a barber.'

This was a bit deflating for Otaké, who had come all prepared to be away from home till the end of the match, in perhaps three months' time. And the Master was in violation of contract. Otaké's annoyance was not soothed by the fact that no one seemed quite sure how clearly the terms had been communicated to the Master. They should have been solemn and inviolable, and that they were broken so soon naturally left Otaké uneasy about the later course of the match. The managers had erred in not explaining them to the Master and explaining them again. No one was prepared to challenge him, however. He was in a class apart, and so the obvious solution was to cajole the young Otaké into continuing play at the Kōyōkan. Otaké proved rather stubborn.

If the Master did not know of the move to Hakoné today, well, that was that. There was a gathering in another room, there were nervous footsteps in the corridors, Otaké disappeared for a long interval. Having nothing better to do, I waited beside the Go board. Soon after what would ordinarily have been lunch time, a compromise was reached: today's session would be from two to four, and with two days' rest the party would go to Hakoné.

'We can't really get started in two hours,' said the Master. 'Let's wait till we get to Hakoné and have a decent session.'

It was a point, but he could not be allowed to have his way. Just such remarks had been responsible for the discord that morning. The spirit of the game should have precluded arbitrary changes in the schedule. The game of Go tended to be controlled these days by inflexible rules. Elaborate conditions had been set for the Master's last game, to keep his old-fashioned wilfulness under control, to deny him a special status, to ensure complete equality.

The system of 'sealing the players in cans' was operative and must be followed through to the end. It was proper that the players go directly from the Kōyōkan to Hakoné. The system meant that they might not leave the appointed site or, lest they receive advice, meet other players until the end of the game. It might be said therefore to guard the sanctity of the contest. It could as well be said to deny human dignity, and yet, in the balance, the integrity and probity of the players were no doubt served. In a match expected to last three months, the sessions to take place at five-day intervals, such precautions seemed doubly necessary. Whatever the wishes of the players themselves, the danger of outside interference was real, and once doubts arose there would be no end to them. The world of Go did of course have its conscience and its ethics, and the likelihood seemed small that there would be talk of a game lasting through multiple sessions, least of all to the players themselves; but again, once an exception was made there would be no end to exceptions.

In the last decade or so of the Master's life he played only three title matches. In all three he fell ill midway through the match. He was bedridden after the first, and after the third he died. All three were eventually finished, but because of recesses the first took two months, the second four, and the third, announced as his last, nearly six months.

The second was held in 1930, five years before the last.[11] Wu of the Fifth Rank was the challenger. The two sides were in delicate balance as the match came into its middle stages, and at about White 150 the Master seemed in a shade the weaker position. Then, at White 160, he made a most extraordinary play, and his second victory was assured. It was rumoured that the play was in fact conceived by Maeda of the Sixth Rank, one of the Master's disciples. Even now the truth is in doubt. Maeda himself has denied the allegation. The game lasted four months, and no doubt the Master's disciples studied it with great care. White 160 may indeed have been invented by one of them, and perhaps, since it was a remarkable invention, someone did pass it on to the Master. Perhaps, again, the play was the Master's own. Only the Master and his disciples know the truth.

The first of the three matches, in 1926, was actually between the Association and a rival group, the Kiseisha, and the generals of the two forces, the Master and Karigané of the Seventh Rank, were in single combat; and there can be little doubt that during the two months it lasted the rival forces put a great deal of study into it. One cannot be sure all the same that they gave advice to their respective leaders. I rather doubt that they did. The Master was not one to ask advice, nor was he an easy man to approach with advice. The solemnity of his art was such as to reduce one to silence.

And even during this his last match there were rumours. Was the recess, ostensibly because of his illness, in fact a stratagem on his part? To me, watching the game through to the end, such allegations were impossible to believe.

It astonished the managers, and myself as well, that Otaké deliberated his first move at Itō, when the game was resumed after a three-month recess, for two hundred and eleven minutes – a full three hours and a half. He began his deliberations at ten thirty in the morning, and with a noon recess of an hour and a half, finally played when the autumn sun was sinking and an electric light hung over the board.

It was at twenty minutes before three that he finally played Black 101.

He looked up laughing. 'See what an idiot I am. It shouldn't have taken me a minute to make the jump. Three and a half hours deciding whether to jump or to push.[12] Ridiculous.' And he laughed again.

The Master smiled wryly and did not answer.

It was as Otaké said: Black 101 was quite obvious to all of

us. The game was entering its decisive stages and the time had come for Black to invade the White formation in the lower right corner; and the point where the play was finally made offered almost the only reasonable beginning. Besides the one-space 'jump' to S-7, the 'push' at S-8 was a possibility; but though some hesitation was understandable the difference was of little account.

Why then did he take so long? Bored with the long wait, I at first thought it merely strange, and then I began to have suspicions. Was it all a show? Was it an irritant, or perhaps a camouflage? I had reasons for these uncharitable suspicions. Play was being resumed after a three-month recess. Had Otaké been studying the board all through those months? At the hundredth play the match was a tight, delicate one. The final stages might have a certain boldness and sweep, but the issue would probably remain in doubt to the end. However often and in whatever formation one lined up the stones there could be no real determination of the outcome. The research and the probing could go on indefinitely. Yet it seemed unlikely that Otaké had abandoned his studies of so important a match. He had had three months in which to think about Black 101. Now to take three and a half hours over the play: might he not be seeking to cover his activities during those three months? The organizers seemed to share my doubts and distaste.

In an interval when Otaké was out of the room, even the Master hinted at dissatisfaction. 'He does take his time,' he muttered. However matters may have been in a practice match, the Master had never before been heard to say anything critical of an opponent during a title match.

But Yasunaga of the Fourth Rank, who was close to both the Master and Otaké, disagreed with me. 'Neither of them seems to have done much of anything during the recess,' he said. 'Otaké is a very fastidious person. He would not want to do anything while the Master was lying helpless in bed.'

Probably it was the truth. Probably in those three hours and a half Otaké was not only deliberating his play; he was bringing himself back to the board after a three-month absence, and doing his best to map out the finished game, through all the stages and formations it was likely to take.

12

It was the Master's first experience with the sealed play. At the beginning of the second session the envelope was brought from the safe of the Kōyōkan, and the seal inspected by the contestants with the secretary of the Association as witness. The contestant who had made the sealed play showed the chart to his adversary, and a stone was placed appropriately on the board. At Hakoné and at Itō the same procedure was followed. The sealed play was in effect a way of hiding from an adversary the last play of a session.

In games lasting over several sessions, it was the custom from ancient times for Black to make the last play of a session, as an act of courtesy towards the more distinguished player. Since the practice gave the advantage to the latter, the injustice was remedied by having the player whose turn it was at the prearranged end of a session, say five o'clock, make the last play. A further refinement was hit upon: to seal the last play. Go took its example from chess, which had first devised the sealed play. The purpose was to eliminate the manifest irrationality of allowing the first player at the beginning of a session, having seen the last play, the whole of the recess, and it could be several days, in which to deliberate his next play, and of not charging the prolonged interval against his allotted time.

It may be said that the Master was plagued in his last match by modern rationalism, to which fussy rules were everything, from which all the grace and elegance of Go as art had disappeared, which quite dispensed with respect for elders and attached no importance to mutual respect as human beings. From the way of Go the beauty of Japan and the Orient had fled. Everything had become science and regulation. The road to advancement in rank, which controlled the life of a player, had become a meticulous point system. One conducted the battle only to win, and there was no margin for remembering the dignity and the fragrance of Go as an art. The modern way was to insist upon doing battle under conditions of abstract justice, even when challenging the Master himself. The fault was not Otaké's. Perhaps what had happened was but natural, Go being a contest and a show of strength.

In more than thirty years the Master had not played Black. He was first among them all, and brooked no second. During his lifetime no one among his juniors advanced as far as the Eighth Rank. All through the epoch that was his own he kept the opposition under control, and there was no one whose rank could carry across the gap to the next age. The fact that today, a decade after the Master's death, no method has been devised for determining the succession to the title Master of Go probably has to do with the towering presence of Honimbō Shūsai. Probably he was the last of the true masters revered in the tradition of Go as a way of life and art.

It begins to seem evident in championship tournaments that the title 'Master' will become a mark of strength and no more, and that the position will become a sort of victory banner and a commercial asset for a competitive performer. It may in fact be said that the Master sold his last match to a newspaper at a price without precedent. He did not so much go forth into combat as allow himself to be lured into combat by the newspaper. It may be that, like the system of certification by schools and teachers in so many of the traditional Japanese arts, the notion of a lifetime Master and of ranks is a feudal relic. It may be that, if he had had to face annual title matches, as do chess masters, the Master would have died years before he did.

In old times the holder of the title, fearful of doing injury to it, seems to have avoided real competition even in practice matches. Never before, probably, was there a master who fought a title match at the advanced age of sixty-four. But in the future the existence of a master who does not play will be unthinkable. Shūsai the Master would seem, in a variety of meanings, to have stood at the boundary between the old and the new. He had at the same time the lofty position of the old master and the material benefits of the new. In a day the spirit of which was a mixture of idolatry and iconoclasm, the Master went into his last match as the last survivor among idols of old.

It was his good fortune to be born in the early flush of Meiji. Probably never again will it be possible for anyone – for, say, Wu Ch'ing-yüan of our own day – knowing nothing of the vale of tears in which the Master spent his student years, to encompass in his individual person a whole panorama of history. It will not be possible even though the man be more of a genius at Go than the Master was. He was the symbol of Go itself, he and his record shining through Meiji, Taishō, and Shōwa, and his achievement in having brought the game to its modern flowering. The match to end the career of the old Master should have had in it the affectionate attention of his juniors, the finesse and subtlety of the warrior's way, the mysterious elegance of an art, everything to make it a masterpiece in itself; but the Master could not stand outside the rules of equality.

When a law is made, the cunning that finds loopholes goes to work. One cannot deny that there is a certain slyness among younger players, a slyness which, when rules are written to prevent slyness, makes use of the rules themselves. In the arsenal are myriad uses of the time allotment and the last play before a recess, the sealed play; and so a Go match as a work of art is besmirched. The Master, when he faced the board, was a man of old. He knew nothing about all these refined latter-day tricks. Through his long competitive career it had been for him the wholly natural thing that the senior in rank should behave arbitrarily, calling a halt to the day's session upon having forced his opponent into an unfortunate play. There was no time allotment. And the arbitrary ways that had been allowed the Master had forged the Master's art, incomparably superior to the latter-day game and all its rules.

The Master was accustomed not to this new equality but to old-fashioned prerogatives, and there had been ugly rumours when the match with Wu of the Fifth Rank had fallen behind schedule; and so it would seem that, in challenging him to this final match, his juniors had imposed the strictest rules to restrain his dictatorial tendencies. The rules for the match had not been set by the Master and Otaké. High-ranking members of the Association had conducted an elimination tournament to decide who would be the challenger, and the code had been drawn up before it began. Otaké, representing the Association, was only trying to make the Master honour the code.

Because of the Master's illness and for other reasons, numbers of disagreements arose, and Otaké's manner, as he repeatedly threatened to forfeit the match, carried suggestions of an inability to understand the courtesies due to an elder, a want of sympathy for a sick man, and a rationalism that somehow missed the point. It caused considerable worry for the managers, and always the technical arguments seemed to be ranged on Otaké's side. There was a possibility, moreover, that giving an inch meant giving a mile, and a possibility too that the slackening of spirit in giving the inch would mean defeat. Such things must not be permitted in so important a contest. Knowing that he had to win, Otaké could not surrender to the whims of his older adversary. It even seemed to me that, when anything suggesting the usual arbitrariness arose, Otaké's insistence on the letter of the law was the more determined for the fact that his opponent was the Master.

The rules were of course very different from those for an ordinary match. Yet it should have been possible to fight without mercy on the board even while making concessions in matters of time and place. There are players capable of such flexibility. The Master perhaps found himself with the wrong adversary.

13

In the world of competitive games, it seems to be the way of the spectator to build up heroes beyond their actual powers. Pitting equal adversaries against each other arouses interest of a sort, but is not the hope really for a nonpareil? The grand figure of 'the invincible Master' towered over the Go board. There had been numerous other battles upon which the Master had staked his destinies, and he had not lost one of them. The results of contests before he gained the title may have been determined by accident and shifting currents. After he became the Master, the world believed that he could not lose, and he had to believe it himself. Therein was the tragedy. By comparison with Sekiné, Master of Shōgi, who was happiest when he lost, Shūsai the Master had a difficult life. One is told that in Go the first player has seven chances in ten of winning, and so it should have been in the nature of things for the Master as White to lose to Otaké; but such refinements are beyond the amateur.

Probably the Master was lured into the game not only by the power of a large newspaper and the size of the fee, but in very great measure too by a real concern for his art. There could be no question that he was consumed by a desire for battle. He probably would not have gone into the match had it occurred to him that he might lose; and it was as if his life ended when the crown of invincibility fell from his head. He had followed his extraordinary destinies through to the end.

Might one perhaps say that following them meant flouting them?

Because the invincible Master, an absolute, was coming forward for the first time in five years, a code unduly complicated even for the day was drawn up. It later came to seem like a foreshadowing of death.

But the code was violated on the day of the second Shiba session, and again immediately after the move to Hakoné.

The move was to take place on 30 June, the third day after the second session. Because of floods it was postponed to 3 July and finally to 8 July. The Kantō was drenched and there were floods in the Kobé region. Even on the eighth the Tōkaidō line was still not through to Osaka. Leaving from Kamakura, I changed at Ofuna for the train on which the Master and his party had come from Tokyo. The 3.15 for Maibara was nine minutes late.

It did not stop at Hiratsuka, where Otaké lived. He promptly appeared at Odawara Station in summer dress, a dark blue suit and a Panama hat turned smartly down at the brim. He was carrying the large suitcase he had brought to the Kōyōkan.

His first business was to inquire about our safety during the floods. 'They still have to use boats to get to the insane asylum down the street from me. At first it was rafts.'

We took the cable car from Miyanoshita down to Dōgashima. The Hayakawa, directly below us, was roiled and muddy. The Taiseikan Inn was like an island in its waters.

After we had been shown to our rooms, Otaké went to make his formal greetings to the Master. In a good mood that evening after his usual cups of saké, the Master talked about this and that, illustrating his remarks liberally with gestures. Otaké spoke of his family and his boyhood. The Master challenged me to a game of Shōgi, and when I seemed reluctant he turned to Otaké instead. The game took almost three and a half hours. Otaké won.

The next morning the Master was being shaved in the corridor outside the bath. He was putting himself in order for tomorrow's session. Because the chair had no headrest, his wife stood behind him supporting his head.

Onoda of the Sixth Rank, who was serving as a judge, and Yawata, the secretary of the Association, arrived that evening. The Master livened the evening with challenges to Shōgi and Ninuki. He lost repeatedly to Onoda at Ninuki, also known as Korean Gomoku.[13] He seemed filled with admiration.

Onoda made a record of a Go match I played with Goi, reporter for the *Nichinichi*. To have a player of the Sixth Rank as recorder was an honour denied even the Master. I played Black and won by five points. A chart of the game appeared in *Kido* (*The Way of Go*), journal of the Association.

It had been agreed that there would be a day to rest from the journey, and that play would be resumed on the tenth. On mornings of play Otaké was a changed man. Tight-mouthed and almost sullen, shoulders back, he paced the halls defiantly. Below the full, somewhat swollen eyelids, the narrow eyes sent forth a fierce light.

But there came a complaint from the Master. Because of the roar of the waters, he said, he had spent two sleepless nights. Reluctantly, he posed for pictures before the Go board, in a room as far as possible from the river. He let it be known that he wished a change of inns.

Insomnia scarcely seemed an adequate reason for postponing a session. The way of Go, moreover, demanded that a player honour his commitments even if his father was dying, even if he seemed on the verge of collapse. The principle still tends to be respected. And to lodge a complaint on the very morning of a session, even if the complainant was the Master himself, showed quite astonishing autocratic tendencies. The match was important for the Master, to be sure, but it was even more important for Otaké.

Since no one among the managers, now and on the earlier

occasion when the Master had broken a promise, was prepared to act as umpire and hand down an order, Otaké must have felt considerable uneasiness about the further course of the match. He quietly acceded to the Master's wishes, however, his face showing scarcely a trace of displeasure.

'I picked the inn myself, and I am very sorry the Master can't sleep,' he said. 'Suppose we find another, and start play tomorrow, after he has had a good night's rest.'

Otaké had stayed at the inn before, and had thought it a good place for a match. Unfortunately the river was so swollen from the rains that boulders came crashing down it, and with the inn situated as if on an island, sleep was indeed difficult. Otaké felt constrained to apologize.

Clad in a cotton summer kimono, he set out with Goi in search of a quiet inn.

14

That morning we moved to the Naraya Inn. The next day, the eleventh, after a recess of some twelve or thirteen days, play was resumed in an outbuilding. The Master lost himself in the game, and his waywardness left him. Indeed he was as quiet and docile as if he had assigned custody of himself to the managers.

The judges for the Master's last match were Onoda and Iwamoto, both of the Sixth Rank. Iwamoto arrived at one on the afternoon of the eleventh. Taking a chair on the veranda, he sat gazing at the mountains. It was the day on which, according to the calendar, the rainy season ended, and indeed the sun was out for the first time in some days. Branches cast shadows over the wet ground, golden carp were bright in the pond. When play began, however, the sky was lightly clouded over once more. There was a strong enough breeze that the flowers in the alcove swayed gently. Aside from the waterfall in the garden and the river beyond, the silence was broken only by the distant sound of a rock-cutter's chisel. A scent of red lilies wafted in from the garden. In the almost too complete silence a bird soared grandly beyond the eaves. There were sixteen plays in the course of the afternoon, from sealed White 12 to sealed Black 27.

After a recess of four days, the second Hakoné session took place on 16 July. The girl who kept the records had always before worn a dark blue kimono speckled with white. Today she had changed to summer dress, a kimono of fine white linen.

This outbuilding was almost a hundred yards across the garden from the main building. The noon recess came, and the figure of the Master going alone down the path caught my eye. Just beyond the gate of the outbuilding was a short slope, and the Master bent forward as he climbed it. I could not see the lines on the palms of the small hands he held lightly clasped behind him, but the network of veins seemed to be complex and delicate. He was carrying a folded fan. His body, bent forward from the hips, was perfectly straight, making his legs seem all the more unreliable. From below the thicket of dwarf bamboo, along the main road, came a sound of water down a narrow ditch. Nothing more – and yet the retreating figure of the Master somehow brought tears to my eyes. I was profoundly moved, for reasons I do not myself understand. In that figure walking absently from the game there was the still sadness of another world. The Master seemed like a relic left behind by Meiji.

'A swallow, a swallow,' he said in a low, husky voice, stopping and looking up into the sky. Beyond him was a stone informing us that the Meiji Emperor had deigned to stay at the inn. The branches of a crape myrtle, not yet in bloom, spread above it. The Naraya had once been a way station for the military aristocracy and their parties.

Onoda came up behind the Master, as if to shield him from something. The Master's wife had come to meet him at the stone bridge over the pond. In the morning and afternoon she would see him as far as the game room, and slip away when he had taken his place at the board. At noon and at the end of a day's session she was always at the pond by their room, waiting for him.

The Master's figure, viewed from the rear, seemed oddly off balance. He had not yet come out of his trance, and the absolutely straight trunk and head were as if he were still at the Go board. He seemed uncertain on his feet. In a state of bemusement, he suggested some rarefied spirit floating over a void; and yet the lines of the figure we saw at the board were still unbroken. They gave off a sort of leftover fragrance, an afterglow.

'A swallow, a swallow.' Perhaps, as the words caught in his throat, the Master was for the first time aware that his posture had not yet returned to normal. So it was with the aged Master. My affection for him, the nostalgia he calls up, come from his power at such times to move me.

15

The first sign from the Master's wife that she was concerned about his health came on 21 July, the day of the third Hakoné session.

'He has been having pains here,' she said, bringing a hand to her chest. He had, it seems, been aware of the trouble since spring.

He had lost his appetite. The day before he had had no breakfast at all, and only a thin slice of toast and a glass of milk for lunch.

During the third session I had noticed the twitching of the hollow cheeks that sagged over the prominent jaws, but I had thought that the heat was affecting him.

That year it went on raining after the rainy season should have ended, and summer was late in coming. Then, before 20 July, when the calendar has summer beginning, it suddenly turned warm. On 21 July a mist hung heavy over Mt Myōjō. The garden was muggy and still. A black swallowtail butterfly hovered among the red lilies, fifteen and sixteen to a stem, at the veranda. Even the flock of crows cawing in the garden seemed warm. Everyone, down to the clerk, was plying a fan. It was the first uncomfortably warm session since the beginning of the match.

'Fierce,' said Otaké, wiping at his forehead and hair with a small towel. 'And Go is fierce too.

> *Up to Hakoné we've come, we've come,*
> *The steepest of them all . . .'[14]*

With time out for lunch, Otaké took three hours and thirty-five minutes to play Black 59.

The Master, his right hand behind him and his left arm on an armrest, was unconcernedly fanning himself with his left hand. From time to time he looked out into the garden. He seemed cool and very much at ease. I could almost feel myself straining with the young Otaké, but the Master's strength seemed quiet, its centre far away.

There were beads of oily sweat on his face, however. Suddenly he brought both hands to his face and pressed at his cheeks. 'It must be fearful in Tokyo.' His mouth was open for some moments afterwards, as if he were remembering the heat of another time, of a distant place.

'Yes,' said Onoda. 'It turned hot very suddenly the day after we went to the lake.' Onoda had just come from Tokyo. On the seventeenth, the day after the preceding session, the Master, Otaké, and Onoda had gone fishing on Lake Ashi.

Three moves followed inevitably when, after long deliberation, Otaké had played Black 59. The stones were as if echoing one another. The situation in the upper reaches of the board was stabilized for the time. The next Black play was a difficult one, the range of possibilities being wide, but Otaké turned to the lower part of the board and played Black 63 after only a moment's thought. He had planned ahead, it seemed, and given himself over to his next assault, a slashing one of the sort that characterized his game. Having dispatched a spy against the White forces below, he returned to the upper part of the board. There was an aggressive impatience in the click of the stone.

'I feel a little cooler now.' Immediately he got up. He left

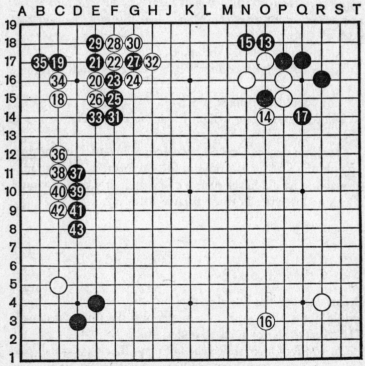

Figure 3: Third and Fourth Sessions (Moves 13–43)

his overskirt in the hall, and when he came out put it on back-wards. 'All backwards. Playing tricks on me. Skirt backwards is tricks, you know.' He righted the error and tied a skilful figure-ten knot. Immediately he was off again, this time to the urinal. 'The heat is worst when you're at the board,' he said, back once more. He wiped vigorously at his glasses with the towel.

It was three in the afternoon. The Master was having an ice. He deliberated for twenty minutes. Apparently Black 63 struck him as a trifle unorthodox.

At the outset of the game, Otaké had been careful to warn the Master that he would frequently ask to be excused; but his departures from the board had been so frequent during the preceding session that the Master had thought them a little odd.

'Is something wrong?' he asked.

'Kidneys. Nerves, really. When I have to think I have to go.'

'You shouldn't drink so much tea.'

'I know. But when I think I want to drink. Excuse me, if you will, please.' And he got up again.

This little way of Otaké's had become material for the gossip columns and the cartoons in the Go journals. The amount of walking he did in the course of a match, it was said, would take him down the Tōkaidō as far as Mishima.

16

Before leaving the board at the end of a session, the players would check the number of moves and the time consumed. The Master was not quick to understand.

On 16 July Otaké sealed the last play, Black 43, at half past four. Informed that there had been a total of sixteen plays in the course of the day, the Master found the statement hard to accept.

'Sixteen? Can we have made that many?'

The girl explained again that from White 28 through the sealed play there had been a total of sixteen. Otaké concurred. The game was still in its early stages and there were only forty-two stones on the board. A glance should had sufficed to confirm the girl's statement, but the Master had his doubts. He counted up stone by stone on his fingers, and still did not seem convinced.

'Let's line them up and see.'

Taking away the stones played that day, he and Otaké replaced them in alternation: one, two, three, and so to sixteen.

'Sixteen?' muttered the Master vacantly. 'Quite a day's work.'

'That's because you're so fast, sir,' said Otaké.

'Oh, but I'm not, though.'

The Master sat absently by the board and showed no inclination to leave. The others could not leave before him.

'Suppose we go on over,' said Onoda after a time. 'You'll feel better.'

'Shall we have a game of Shōgi?' said the Master, looking up as if he had just been awakened. There was nothing feigned about this air of abstraction.

A mere sixteen plays scarcely demanded a recount, and a player has the whole of the board constantly in his head, when he is eating and even when he is sleeping. Perhaps it was a sign of dedication and a concern for precision that the Master all the same insisted on replaying each of the stones, and would not be satisfied until he had done so. Perhaps too it had in it a certain element of circumspection. One saw in the curious mannerism the loneliness of an old man who has not had too happy a life.

At the fifth session five days later, 21 July, there were twenty-two plays, from White 44 to the sealed Black 65.

'How much time did I use?' the Master asked the girl.

'An hour and twenty minutes.'

'That much?' He seemed incredulous. The total time he had used for his eleven plays was six minutes fewer than Otaké had used for Black 59 alone. Yet he seemed to think he had played more rapidly.

'It does seem unlikely that you used so much time, sir,' said Otaké. 'You were playing at a fearful rate.'

'How much for the *bōshi*?'[15] the Master asked the girl.

'Sixteen minutes.'

'The *tsuki-atari*?'[16]

'Twenty minutes.'

'The link took you longer,' said Otaké.

'White 58 that would be?' The girl looked at her records. 'Thirty-five minutes.'

The Master still did not seem convinced. He took the chart from the girl and examined it intently.

I like a good bath, and it was summer; and always when a session ended I went immediately to the bath house. Today Otaké was almost as quick as I was.

'You made good progress.'

'The Master is fast and he makes no mistakes, and that gives him a double advantage,' laughed Otaké. 'The game is as good as over.'

I could still feel the strength that seemed to flow from him when he was at the board. It was something of an embarrassment to meet a Go player just before or after a session.

This restless energy suggested great resolve. Branded on his mind, perhaps, was a plan for a violent attack.

Onoda of the Sixth Rank too was astonished at the Master's speed.

'Eleven hours would be more than enough for him even in a grand tournament. But it's a difficult spot. That *bōshi* isn't the kind of play you make in a hurry.'

Through the fourth session, on 16 July, White had used four

hours and thirty-eight minutes, and Black six hours and fifty-two minutes. At the end of the fifth session, on 21 July, the difference was even greater: five hours and fifty-seven minutes for White, ten hours and twenty-eight minutes for Black.

At the end of the sixth session, on 31 July,[17] White had used eight hours and thirty-two minutes, Black twelve hours and forty-three minutes; and at the end of the seventh on 5 August, White had used ten hours and thirty-one minutes, Black fifteen hours and forty-five minutes.

But by the tenth session, on 14 August, the distance had narrowed: White had used fourteen hours and fifty-eight minutes as against Black's seventeen hours and forty-seven minutes. It was on that day, after sealing White 100, that the Master went into St Luke's Hospital. Struggling bravely on despite his illness, he had used two hours and seven minutes for a single play, White 90, on 5 August.

When finally the match ended on 4 December, there was an uncomfortable difference of some fourteen or fifteen hours between the two. Shūsai the Master had used nineteen hours and fifty-seven minutes, and Otaké of the Seventh Rank had used thirty-four hours and nineteen minutes.

17

Nineteen hours and fifty-seven minutes would be very near the time allotted both players in an ordinary match, but the Master still had more than twenty hours left. Otaké with his thirty-four hours and nineteen minutes still had almost six hours.

The Master's White 130 was the careless play that proved fatal. If he had not made the mistake, and if the match had continued with the two sides generally equal or the advantage for the one or the other very small, it seems likely that Otaké would have hung on until he had used the whole of his forty hours. After White 130, he knew that he had won.

Both the Master and Otaké were famous for tenacity, and both were given to long deliberation. Otaké would wait until most of his time was gone; and his way of making a hundred and more plays in the last minutes gave his game its own peculiar ferocity. The Master, disciplined in an age when there were no time restrictions, was not capable of such a *tour de force*. Indeed he had probably insisted upon forty hours so that the last battle of his life might be quite free from the pressures of time.

The time allotment in the Master's title matches had always been large. It was sixteen hours when in 1926 he played Karigané of the Seventh Rank. Karigané lost because he ran out of time, but a victory by five or six points for the Master's White seemed unshakable. Indeed there were those who said that Karigané should have played like a man, and not allowed insufficient time to be the excuse for his defeat. When the Master played Wu of the Fifth Rank, twenty-four hours were allotted each player.

For the Master's retirement match, the time was about double that for even these unusually long matches, and four times that for an ordinary match. Time restrictions could as well have been dispensed with.

If this extraordinary time allotment was made at the Master's behest, then it may be said that he took upon himself a heavy burden. He had to endure both his own illness and long periods of meditation on the part of his adversary. Those thirty-four hours should argue the case convincingly enough.

Again, the arrangement to play every fifth day was out of deference to the Master's age; but in fact it added to the burden. If both sides had used the allotted time to the full, a total of eighty hours, and each session had lasted five hours, then there would have been a total of sixteen sessions – which is to say that even if the match had proceeded without interruption it would have lasted some three months. Anyone who knows the spirit of Go knows too that the required concentration cannot be maintained or the tension endured for three whole months. They mean something akin to a whittling away of the player's physical being. The Go board is with a player waking and sleeping, and a four-day recess therefore meant not rest but exhaustion.

The recesses became even more trying after the Master fell ill. The Master himself, of course, and the managers as well, wanted to be finished with the match on the earliest day possible. He must be allowed to rest, and there was a danger that he might collapse along the way.

He had even said to his wife, she told me sadly, that he no longer cared who won, he only wanted to be finished with it all.

'And not once before in his whole life has he said that sort of thing.'

'He won't improve as long as the match goes on,' one of the managers is reported to have said, his head bowed. 'I've sometimes thought he might do well just to throw it over. But of course he couldn't. His art means too much to him. I haven't really taken the possibility seriously, of course. It's just a thought that comes to me at bad moments.'

It may have been a professional remark of a confidential nature, but the moments must have been very bad ones indeed. The Master himself had not once been heard to complain. Indeed through his competitive career of a half century he had probably won a considerable number of games by being a very little more patient than his adversary. Nor was the Master one to exaggerate his unhappiness or discomfort.

18

Once shortly after play was resumed at Itō I asked the Master whether he meant to return to St Luke's Hospital when the match was over, or winter as usual in Atami.

'The question is whether I last that long,' he said, as if taking me into his confidence. 'It seems strange that I've come as far as I have. I'm not much of a thinker, and I don't have what you might call beliefs. People talk about my responsibility to the game, but that hasn't been enough to bring me this far. And they can call it physical strength if they like – but that really isn't it either.' He spoke slowly, his head slightly bowed. 'Maybe I have no nerves. A vague, absent sort – maybe the vagueness has been good for me. The word means two different things in Tokyo and in Osaka, you know. In Tokyo it means stupidity, but in Osaka they talk about vagueness in a painting and in a game of Go. That sort of thing.' The Master seemed to savour the word as he spoke, and I savoured it as I listened.

It was not like the Master to discuss his feelings so openly. He was not one to show emotion on his face or in his speech. More than once through my long hours of observing the match, I had suddenly felt that I was savouring a quite ordinary word or gesture of the Master's.

Hirotsuki Zekken, who had been the Master's faithful supporter since 1908, when he succeeded to the title Honimbō, and who had collaborated in his writings, once wrote that in more than thirty years of service he had not received a single word of thanks from the Master. He had mistakenly taken the Master for a chilly, unfeeling man, he added. And when people said that the Master was using Zekken, the Master is said to have responded with lordly indifference, as if to say that the question was not of a sort that he chose to concern himself with. Reports that the Master was not very clean in financial matters were also mistaken, said Zekken, and he could offer ample evidence to refute them.

Nor did the Master offer anyone a word of thanks during his retirement match. His wife took responsibility for such niceties. He was not presuming upon his rank and title. He was being himself.

When professionals in the Go world came to him with problems, he would grunt and fall silent, and it was very difficult indeed to guess his views. Since one could hardly press a point upon so exalted a person, he must have been a source of much uncertainty, I sometimes thought. His wife would act as aide and moderator, seeking to temper his unconditional silence.

This somewhat dull and insensitive side of his nature, the slowness of apprehension that he himself had called 'vagueness', was very apparent in his hobbies and diversions. In Shōgi and Renju of course, and in billiards and mahjong as well, he was the despair of his adversaries for the time he spent in thought.

He played billiards a number of times with Otaké and myself during our stay in Hakoné. He would score perhaps seventy if the other player were generous. Otaké kept careful tally, as became a professional. 'Forty-two for me, fourteen for Wu . . .'

The Master would think out each stroke at his leisure, and after he had taken up his position he would draw the cue endlessly back and forth through his hand. One tends to think that in billiards good form depends upon the speed of the flow from shoulder and arm to billiard ball, but in the case of the Master there was no such flow at all. One quite lost patience as he slipped the cue back and forth. But, watching, I would feel a kind of sadness and affection.

When he played mahjong he would line up his tiles on a

long, narrow piece of white paper. Taking the neatness of the folded paper and the row of tiles as a mark of the Master's fastidiousness, I once asked him about it.

'Yes. They're clearer and easier to see when you have them on white paper. Try it sometime.'

In mahjong too the key to victory is supposed to be brisk, quick play; but the Master deliberated each move at length. His adversaries, pushed beyond boredom, would presently flag and fall. Lost in his own game, the Master was quite oblivious of the feelings of others. He was not even aware of the fact that he sometimes dragged people kicking and struggling into a game.

19

'You do not learn about your opponent's character when you play Go or when you play Shōgi,' the Master once remarked, apropos of amateur Go. 'Trying to judge your opponent's character perverts the whole spirit of the game.' Presumably he was annoyed at amateur theoreticians of Go. 'I lose myself in the game, and my opponent stops mattering.'

On 2 January 1940, which is to say a half month before his death, the Master participated in the game of Team Go that officially opened the year for the Go Association. The players who assembled at the Association offices made five plays each, the equivalent of leaving their calling cards. Since the wait seemed likely to be a long one, a second game was started. The Master took his place opposite Seo of the Second Rank, who had no other partner, at White 20 of the second game. They made their five plays each, from Black 21 to White 30. There being no others to follow, the game was to be suspended at White 30. Even so, the Master spent forty minutes thinking about his last play. He was the last to appear in what was after all a ceremonial observance, and he could as well have made his play immediately and been done with the matter.

I went to see him at St Luke's Hospital during the three-month recess in his retirement match. The furnishings were huge, to fit the American physique. There was something precarious about the Master's small figure perched on the lofty bed. The dropsical swelling had largely gone from his face, and his cheeks were somewhat fuller; but more striking was a certain lightness in the figure, as if he had thrown off a heavy spiritual burden. He seemed carefree and almost lackadaisical, a different old gentleman from the Master at the Go board.

A reporter from the *Nichinichi* chanced to be visiting him too. The competitions, he said, had proved extremely popular. Every Saturday readers were invited to submit opinions as to how at certain crucial points the match should proceed.

'This week's problem is Black 91,' I ventured to add.

'Black 91?' The expression on the Master's face was as if he were gazing at a Go board.

I regretted my remark. One was not to talk about Go. But I went on to explain: 'White jumps one space, and Black plays on the diagonal away from himself.'

'Oh, that. But there's nothing for him to do but play next to his own stone either on the horizontal or on the diagonal. I imagine plenty of people will come up with the answer.' As he spoke he brought himself into an upright kneeling position, knees together, head up. It was his posture at the Go board. There was a cold, severe dignity in it. For a time it was as if, face to face with a void, he had lost all consciousness of his own identity.

It did not seem, now or at the team match, that devotion to his art made him take each move so seriously, or that he was overdoing his responsibilities as the Master. It seemed rather that what must happen was happening.

When a younger player was trapped into a game with the

Master, he was left quite exhausted at the end of it. There was, for example, a one-lance handicap Shōgi game[18] he played with Otaké during our stay at Hakoné: it lasted from ten in the morning until six in the evening. Then there was a Shōgi game during a three-match Go contest between Otaké and Wu, sponsored by this same *Tokyo Nichinichi*. The Master did the commentary and I was reporter for the second match. The Master forced Fujisawa Kuranosuké of the Fifth Rank, who also happened to be present, into a game of chess which lasted from noon through the afternoon and evening and on until three in the morning. The moment he saw Fujisawa the next day, the Master pulled out his chess board again. So it was with the Master.

We had gathered the night before the second Hakoné session. 'The Master is astonishing,' said Sunada, a *Nichinichi* Go reporter who was acting as a sort of factotum for the Master. 'On every one of these last four days when he is supposed to have been resting, he has come around first thing in the morning and challenged me to a game of billiards. We've played all day long and on into the night, every single day. He's not just a genius. He's inhuman.'

The Master had not once, it is said, complained to his wife of weariness from competitive play. There is a story she likes to tell of his ability to sink himself into a game. I myself heard it at the Naraya.

'We were living at Kōgai-chō in Azabu. It wasn't a very big house, and he had matches and practice in a ten-mat room. The trouble was that the eight-mat room next door was the parlour. Sometimes we had rather noisy guests. He was having a match one day with I don't remember who when my sister came by to show me her new baby. Babies will be babies, and it cried the whole of the time. I was frantic and only wished she would go away; but I hadn't seen her for a very long time, and she had come for a very special reason, and I couldn't tell her to go. When she did finally leave, I went to apologize for all the noise. And do you know he hadn't heard a thing! He hadn't known she was there, and hadn't heard the baby.' And she added: 'Ogishi used to say that he wanted as soon as he possibly could to be like the Master. Every night before he went to sleep he would sit up in bed and meditate. There was the Okada school of meditation in those days, you know.'

The Ogishi she referred to was Ogishi Sōji of the Sixth Rank, so outstanding a pupil that he was said to have had a monopoly on the Master's trust and confidence and the Master had thought of making him heir to the title Honimbō. He died in January 1924, at the age of twenty-seven by the Oriental count. The Master in his last years was constantly being reminded of Ogishi.

Nozawa Chikuchō has similar stories of how, during his days in the Fourth Rank, he would have games at the Master's house. Off in the houseboy's room some very young disciples who were living with the Master were one day making a stir that could be heard in the game room itself. Nozawa went off to caution them. They were certain to be scolded by the Master, he said. But the Master, it appeared, had heard nothing.

20

'All through lunch he sat gazing off into space,' said his wife. 'He must have been in a difficult spot.' It was 26 July, the day of the fourth Hakoné session. 'I told him it wouldn't do. If he went on eating as if he didn't know he was eating, his stomach would rebel. I told him he would ruin his digestion if he didn't put himself into a mood for it. He frowned and went on looking off into space.'

The Master apparently had not expected the violent attack that came with Black 69. He deliberated his response for an hour and forty-six minutes. It was his slowest play since the beginning of the match.

But Otaké had probably been planning Black 69 all through the recess. At the beginning of the session he reread the situation for twenty minutes, as if restraining an impulse towards haste. He seemed to exude strength, he swayed violently, he thrust a knee towards the board. Briskly he played Black 67 and Black 69. Then he laughed a high laugh.

'A thunder storm? A tempest?'

Dark clouds were blowing up. There was rain on the lawn, and then rain against the glass doors that had hastily been pulled shut. Otaké's jest was of a sort he was much given to, but it had the sound of fulfilment as well.

An expression flickered across the Master's face as of astonishment or foreboding, and at the same time as of feigned bewilderment, meant to please and amuse. Even so ambiguous an expression was unusual for the Master.

Black made a very curious play during the sessions at Itō, a sealed play that seemed to take advantage of the fact that it was a sealed play. The Master could scarcely wait for the recess to let his indignation be known. He thought that the game had been sullied and he was on the point of forfeiting. Seated at the board, however, he had not let his face reveal a trace of his feelings. No one among the spectators could have guessed their intensity.

Black 69 was like the flash of a dagger. The Master fell into silent thought, and the time came for the noon recess. Otaké stood beside the board even after the Master had left.

'Now we're in for it,' he said. 'This is the divide.' He continued to look down at the board as if unable to tear himself away.

'A little unkind of you?' I said.

'He's always making *me* do the thinking.' Otaké laughed brightly.

But the Master played White 70 as soon as he returned from

lunch. It was all too clear that he had made use of the noon recess, not charged against his time allotment; but the trickery was not in the Master to conceal the misdemeanour by pretending to deliberate his first afternoon play. The penalty was that he had spent the recess gazing into space.

21

That aggressive Black 69 has been described as 'a diabolic stroke'. The Master himself said afterwards that it had the sort of ferocity Otaké was known for. Everything depended upon the White response. If it proved inadequate, White could quite easily have lost control of the board. The Master deliberated an hour and forty-six minutes over White 70. His longest period of meditation came ten days later, on 5 August, when he spent two hours and seven minutes on White 90. White 70 was his second slowest play.

If Black 69 was diabolically aggressive, White 70 was a brilliant holding play. Onoda, among others, was speechless with admiration. The Master stood firm and averted a crisis. He retreated a pace and forestalled disaster. A magnificent play, it cannot have been easy to make. Black had charged into a headlong assault, and with this one play White had turned it back. Black had made gains, and yet it seemed that White, casting away the dressings from his wounds, had emerged with greater lightness and freedom of action.

The sky was dark with the squall Otaké had called a tempest, and the lights were on. The white stones, reflected on the mirrorlike face of the board, became one with the figure of the Master, and the violence of the wind and rain in the garden seemed to intensify the stillness of the room.

The squall soon passed. A mist trailed over the mountain,

and the sky brightened from the direction of Odawara, down the river. The sun struck the rise beyond the valley, locusts shrilled, the glass doors at the veranda were opened again. Four black puppies were sporting on the lawn as Otaké played Black 73. Once more the sky was lightly clouded over.

There had been showers early in the morning. Seated on the veranda, Kumé Masao had said at the morning session: 'What a feeling it gives a person just to be sitting here.' His voice was soft but intense. 'A clean, transparent feeling.'

Kumé, who had recently become literary editor for the *Nichinichi*, had stayed over to be present at the session. He was the first novelist in many years to become a literary editor. Go fell within his jurisdiction.

He knew almost nothing about Go. He would sit on the veranda, now looking at the mountains and now looking at the players. Psychic waves seemed to come to him from the players all the same. The Master would be sunk in anguished thought, and an expression of anguish would cross Kumé's good-natured face.

I could not pretend to know much more about Go than Kumé did; but even so it seemed to me that the unmoving stones, as I gazed at them from the side of the board, spoke to me as living creatures. The sound of the stones on the board seemed to echo vastly through another world.

The game site was an outbuilding, three rooms in a row, one of ten mats and two of nine. There were *nemu* blossoms in the alcove of the ten-mat room.

'They seem ready to fall,' said Otaké.

White 80 was the sealed play, and the fifteenth of the day. The Master did not seem to hear the girl's warning that four o'clock, the hour appointed for the end of the session, was near. She hesitated, leaning slightly forward.

'You will seal your play, please, sir, if you don't mind,' said Otaké in her place, as if shaking a drowsy child.

The Master seemed, at length, to hear. He muttered something to himself. His voice caught in his throat, and I do not know what he said. Thinking that the sealed play would have been decided upon, the secretary of the Association readied an envelope; but the Master sat vacantly on, as if apart from the matter at hand.

'I haven't decided,' he said finally. The expression on his face was as of having been away from reality and not being able to return quite yet.

He deliberated sixteen minutes longer. White 80 took forty-four minutes.

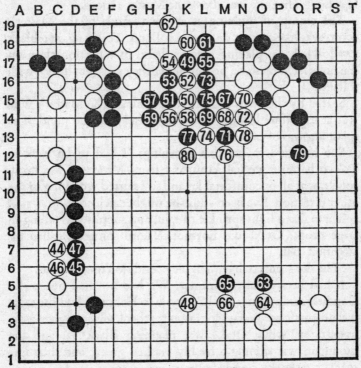

Figure 4: Fifth and Sixth Sessions (Moves 44–80)

22

On 31 July play was moved to yet another suite, called the 'new upper rooms', a row of three rooms once more, two of eight mats and one of six. The framed inscriptions on the walls were in the hands of Rai Sanyō, Yamaoka, Tesshū, and Yoda Gakkai.[19] The suite was above the Master's room.

The clump of hydrangeas at the veranda of the Master's room was like a great distended balloon. Today again a black swallowtail was playing among them, its reflection clean on the pond. The wisteria bower under the eaves was heavy with foliage.

Seated by the board, I heard a splashing. The Master's wife was at the stone bridge, throwing bread into the pond. The splashing was of carp come to feed.

She had said to me that morning: 'I had to be back in Tokyo because we had company from Kyoto. It was fairly cool, not at all uncomfortable; and so I started worrying in the other direction. I've been afraid he might catch cold.'

There was a light sprinkle of rain, and soon it was falling in large drops. Otaké did not notice until someone called his attention to it.

'The sky seems to have a kidney condition too,' he said.

It had been a rainy summer. We had not had one really cloudless session since we had come to Hakoné. And the rains were capricious. Today, for instance, there was sunlight on the hydrangeas while Otaké was planning Black 83, and the mountain was shining a freshly washed green, and then immediately the sky clouded over again.

Black 83 took even longer, an hour and forty-eight minutes, than White 70. Gazing intently at the right side of the board,

Otaké pushed himself a shin's length away, cushion and all. Then he put his hands inside his kimono and, shoulders back, seemed to brace himself. It was his signal that a long period of deliberation had begun.

The match was entering its middle phases. Every play was a difficult one. It was fairly clear which territories White and Black had staked out, and the time was approaching when a calculation of the final score might be possible. Proceed immediately into a final showdown, invade enemy ground, challenge to close-in fighting somewhere on the board? – the time had come for a summing up, and for projecting the phases to come.

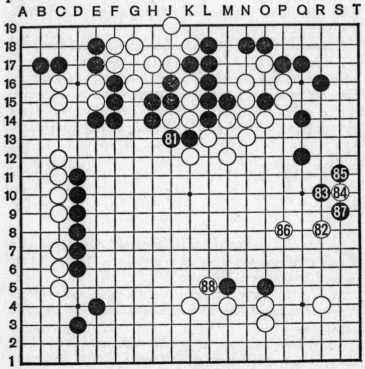

Figure 5: Seventh Session (Moves 81–88)

Dr Felix Dueball, who had learned Go in Japan and gone back to Germany, and who was known as 'the German Honimbō', sent the Master a congratulatory telegram on the occasion of his retirement match. A picture of the two players reading the telegram had been in the morning's *Nichinichi*.

White 88 was the sealed play of the session.

Yawata of the Association promptly found significance in the fact. 'You are being congratulated, sir, on your lucky number,'[20] he said.

The Master's face and neck, which one would have thought could be no thinner, seemed thinner by the day. Yet he seemed in better health than on that hot 16 July, and in the best of spirits. Might one say that with a falling away of the flesh the bones beneath are stronger?

None of us foresaw his near collapse a scant five days later.

But he stood up abruptly, as if he could wait no longer, when Otaké had played Black 83. All his exhaustion came suddenly to the surface. It was twenty-seven minutes after twelve, and of course time for the noon recess; but the Master had not before left the board as if kicking it away from him.

23

'I have prayed and prayed that this would not happen,' the Master's wife said to me on the morning of 5 August. 'I have been of too little faith, I suppose.'

And again: 'I was afraid this might happen, and maybe it happened because I worried too much. There is nothing to do now but pray.'

The curious and attentive combat reporter, I had had the whole of my attention on the Master as hero in battle; and now the words of the wife who had been with him through the long years came to me as if striking a blind spot. I could think of no answer.

The long, strenuous match had aggravated the heart condition from which he had long suffered, and apparently the pain in his chest had for some days been intense. He had let slip not a word about it.

From early in August his face began to swell and the chest pains were worse.

A session was scheduled for 5 August. It was decided that play be limited to two hours in the morning. The Master was to be examined before it began.

'The doctor?' he asked.

The doctor had gone to Sengokuhara on an emergency case.

'Well, suppose we begin, then.'

Seated at the board, the Master quietly took up a tea bowl in both hands and sipped at the strong brew. Then he folded his hands lightly on his knees and brought himself upright. The expression on his face was like that of a child about to weep. The tightly closed lips were thrust forward, there was a dropsical swelling in the cheeks, and the eyelids too were swollen.

The session began almost on schedule, at seven minutes past ten. Today again a mist turned to heavy rain. Then, presently, the sky was brighter from downstream.

White 88, the sealed play, was opened. Otaké played Black 89 at forty-eight minutes past the hour. Noon came, an hour and a half passed, and still the Master had not decided on White 90. In great physical discomfort, he took an extraordinary two hours and seven minutes for the play. The whole time he sat bolt upright. The swelling seemed to leave his face. Finally it was decided to recess for lunch.

The usual one-hour recess was extended to two hours, in the course of which the Master was examined.

Otaké reported that he too was indisposed. His digestion was troubling him. He was taking three stomach medicines

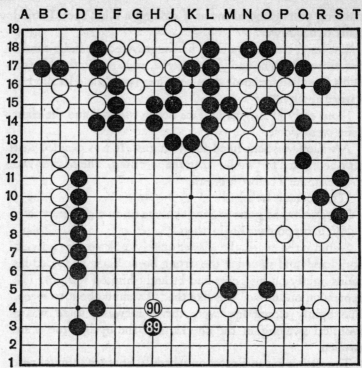

Figure 6: Eighth Session (Moves 89 and 90)

and a medicine to prevent fainting as well. He had been known to faint during a match.

'It usually happens when I'm playing badly, when I'm running out of time, and when I'm not feeling well,' he said. 'He insists on playing. I would as soon not, myself.'

The Master's sealed White 90 had been decided upon when they returned to the board.

'You must be exhausted,' said Otaké.

'I'm sorry. I've been very demanding.' It was not usual for the Master to apologize.

So the day's session ended.

'The swelling doesn't worry me a great deal,' he explained

to Kumé, literary editor of the *Nichinichi*. 'It's all the things that are going on in here.' He drew a circle over his chest. 'I have trouble breathing, and I have palpitations, and sometimes it feels as though a huge weight were pressing down on me. I like to think of myself as young. But I've been very conscious of the years since I turned fifty.'

'It would be good if a fighter could fight off the years,' said Kumé.

'I'm feeling the years already, sir,' said Otaké, 'and I'm only thirty.'

'That's a bit soon,' said the Master.

For a time the Master sat in the anteroom with Kumé and several others. He talked of old times, of how as a boy he had gone to Kobé and at a naval review seen electric lights for the first time.

'I've been forbidden to play billiards.' He got up laughing. 'But a little Shōgi is permitted. Let's be at it.'

The Master's 'little' was not likely to be very little.

'Maybe we should make it mahjong,' said Kumé, challenged to yet another battle. 'You don't have to use your head so much.'

The Master had only porridge and a salted plum for lunch.

24

No doubt Kumé had come because word of the Master's illness had reached Tokyo. Maeda Nobuaki of the Sixth Rank, a disciple of the Master's, was also present. The judges, Onoda and Iwamoto, both of the Sixth Rank, were in attendance that 5 August. Takagi, Master of Renju, stopped by on his way through Hakoné, and Doi, Shōgi player of the Eighth Rank, who was staying at Miyanoshita, came calling too. There were games all through the inn.

The Master took Kumé's advice and settled for mahjong, the others in the foursome being Kumé himself, Iwamoto, and Sunada, reporter for the *Nichinichi*. The others played as gingerly as if they were cleaning a wound, but the Master, as always, quite lost himself in the game. Alone among the four, he spent long periods in meditation.

'Please,' said his wife uneasily. 'If you overdo it your face will swell up again.'

He did not seem to hear.

I was learning Mobile Renju[21] from Takagi Rakuzan, Master of Renju. Skilful at all manner of games and adept at inventing new games as well, Takagi enlivened any gathering. I learned of his ideas for a puzzle to be called 'cloistered maiden'.[22]

After dinner and far into the night, the Master played Ninuki Renju[23] with Yawata of the Go Association and Goi of the *Nichinichi*.

Maeda left in the afternoon, after a brief conversation with the Master's wife. Since the Master was his teacher and Otaké his brother-in-law, he feared misunderstanding and rumours, and so avoided the two players. And perhaps he remembered rumours that he had devised the remarkable White 160 in the Master's game with Wu.

On the morning of the sixth, through the good offices of the *Nichinichi*, Dr Kawashima came from Tokyo to examine the Master. The valve at the aorta was not closing properly.

No sooner was the examination over than the Master, sitting up in bed, was at Shōgi again. Onoda was his partner, and he was using the 'unpromoted-silver' offensive.[24] Afterwards Onoda and Takagi, Master of Renju, had a game by the Korean rules.[25] The Master, propped against an armrest, looked on.

'Now we'll have a game of mahjong,' he said, as if scarcely able to await the outcome. Since I did not know mahjong, however, they were one man short.

'Mr Kumé?' said the Master.
'Mr Kumé is seeing the doctor back to Tokyo.'
'Mr Iwamoto?'
'He's gone back too.'
'Gone back,' echoed the Master weakly. I found his disappointment most touching.

I myself was going back to Karuizawa

25

Upon consultation with concerned persons on the newspaper and in the Go Association, it was decided that Dr Kawashima of Tokyo and Dr Okajima of Miyanoshita would follow the Master's wishes and permit the match to continue. Their conditions were that, to ease the strain on the Master, the five-hour sessions every fifth day be replaced by sessions half as long every third or fourth day. The Master was to be examined before and after every session.

It was no doubt a last resort, this plan to have the match over in fewer days and leave the Master to convalesce. Accommodations at a hot-spring resort all through a match lasting two or three months may seem like a great luxury. For the players, however, the system of 'sealing in cans' was exactly that: they were sealed in tightly with the game of Go. Had they been allowed to return home during the four-day recesses, they might have left the Go board behind and taken their minds from it, and so been able to rest; imprisoned on the site, they had few diversions. There would have been no problem had the 'canning' been a matter of a few days or a week, but keeping the sixty-four-year-old Master imprisoned for two and three months must be described as torture. Canning is the usual practice today. Little thought was given to the evils compounded by the Master's age and the length of the match. To the Master himself the somewhat pompous rules may have seemed the equivalent of a laurel crown.

The Master collapsed in less than a month.

At this late date the rules were to be changed. For Otaké the matter was of grave import. If the Master could not respect the original contract, then the honourable thing would be to forfeit.

Otaké could not say exactly that, but he did lodge a complaint. 'I can't get enough rest in three days, and I can't get into my stride in only two and a half hours.'

He conceded the point, but the contest with an ailing old man put him in a difficult position. 'I don't want it to be said that I forced a sick man to play. I would as soon not play myself, and he insists on it; but I can't expect people to understand. It's as sure as anything can be that they'll take the other view. If we go on with the match and his heart condition is worse, then everyone will blame me. A fine thing, really. I'll be remembered as someone who left a smear on the history of the game. And out of ordinary humanity, shouldn't we let him take all the time he needs to recover and then have our game?'

He seemed to mean, in sum, that it was not easy to play with a man who obviously was very ill. He would not want it thought that he had taken advantage of the illness to win, and his position would be even worse if he lost. The outcome was still not clear. The Master was able to forget his own illness when he sat down at the board, and Otaké, struggling himself to forget, was at a disadvantage. The Master had become a tragic figure. The newspaper had quoted him to the effect that the Go player's ultimate desire was to collapse over the board. He had become a martyr, sacrificing himself to his art. The nervous, sensitive Otaké had to struggle on as if indifferent to his opponent's trials.

Even the *Nichinichi* reporters said the issue had become one of ordinary humanity. Yet it was the *Nichinichi*, sponsor of this retirement match, that wanted it at all costs to go on. The match was being serialized and had become enormously popular. My reports were doing well too, followed even by persons who knew nothing of Go. There were those who suggested to me that the Master hated the thought of losing that enormous fee. I thought them somewhat too imaginative.

On the night before the next session, scheduled for 10 August, an effort was mounted to overcome Otaké's objections. A certain childish perverseness in Otaké made him say no when others said yes, and a certain obduracy kept him from assenting when assent seemed the obvious thing; and then the newspaper reporters and the functionaries of the Go Association were not good persuaders. No solution was at hand. Yasunaga Hajimé of the Fourth Rank was a friend who knew the workings of Otaké's mind, and he had had much experience at mediating disputes. He stepped forward to make Otaké see reason; but this dispute proved too much for him.

Late in the night Mrs Otaké came with her baby from Hiratsuka. She wept as she argued with her husband. Her speech was warm and gentle and without a trace of disorder even as she wept; nor was there a suggestion in her manner of the virtuous wife seeking to edify and reform. Her tearful plea was quite sincere. I looked on with admiration.

Her father kept a hot-spring inn at Jigokudani in Shinshū. The story of how Otaké and Wu shut themselves up at Jigokudani to study new openings is famous in the Go world. I myself had long known of Mrs Otaké's beauty, indeed since she was a girl. A young poet coming down from Shiga Heights had taken note of the beautiful sisters at Jigokudani and passed on his impressions to me.

I was caught a little off balance by the dutiful, somewhat drab housewife I saw at Hakoné; and yet in the figure of the mother quite given over to domestic duties, which allowed little time to worry about her own appearance, I could still see the pastoral beauty of her mountain girlhood. The gentle sagacity was immediately apparent. And I thought I had never seen so splendid a baby. In that boy of eight months was such strength and vigour that I thought I could see a certain epic quality in Otaké himself. The boy had clear, delicate skin.

Even now, twelve and thirteen years later, she speaks each time I see her of 'the boy you were so kind as to praise'. And I understand that she says to the boy himself: 'Do you remember the nice things Mr Uragami said about you in his newspaper articles?'

Otaké was persuaded by his wife's remarks. His family was important to him.

He agreed to play, but he lay awake all night. He went on worrying. At five or six in the morning he was pacing the halls. I saw him early in the morning, already in formal clothes, lying on a sofa by the entrance.

26

There was no radical change in the Master's condition on the tenth, and the doctors allowed the session to proceed. Yet his cheeks were swollen, and it was clear to all of us that he was weaker. Asked whether the session should be in the main building or one of the outbuildings, he said that he could no longer walk. Since Otaké had earlier complained about the waterfall by the main building, however, he would defer to Otaké's wishes. The waterfall was artificial, and so the decision was that it should be turned off and the session held in the main building. At the Master's words I felt a surge of sadness that was akin to anger.

Lost in the game, the Master seemed to give over custody of his physical self. He left everything to the managers, and made no demands. Even during the great debate over the effects of his illness upon the game, the Master himself had sat absently apart, as if it did not concern him.

The moon had been bright on the night of the ninth, and in the morning the sunlight was strong, the shadows were clean, the white clouds bright. It was the first true midsummer weather since the beginning of the match. The leaves of the *nemu* were open their fullest. The pure white of Otaké's cloak-string caught the eye.

'Isn't it nice that the weather has settled,' remarked the Master's wife. But a change had come over her face.

Mrs Otaké too was pale from lack of sleep. The two wives hovered near their husbands, the eyes in the worn faces alive with open disquiet. They looked too like women who no longer sought to hide their egoism.

The midsummer light was powerful. Against it the Master's figure took on a darkened grandeur. The spectators sat with heads bowed, not really looking at the Master. Otaké, so given to jesting, was silent today.

Must play go on even in this extremity I asked myself, grieving for the Master. What was this something called Go? As death was approaching, the novelist Naoki Sanjūgo wrote what was for him a curiosity, an autobiographical story called 'I'. He said that he envied the Go player. 'If one chooses to look upon Go as valueless,' he said, 'then absolutely valueless it is; and if one chooses to look upon it as a thing of value, then a thing of absolute value it is.'

'Are you ever lonely?' he asked the owl on the table before him. The owl turned to destroying a newspaper which carried an account of the Master's game with Wu, recessed because of the Master's illness. Naoki sought to examine the worth of his own popular writings in the light of the strong fascination Go had for him, and its world of pure competition.

'I am very tired. I must write thirty pages by nine this evening and it is now past four. I do not really care. I think I may be allowed to waste a day on an owl. How little I have worked for myself, how much for journalism and other encumbering forces. And how coldly they have treated me!'

He wrote himself to death. Through him I first met the Master and Wu.

There had been something ghostlike about Naoki in his last days, and there was something ghostlike about the Masters here before me.

Yet the game moved ahead nine plays during the session. It was Otaké's turn at twelve-thirty, the hour appointed for the recess. The Master left the board. Otaké stayed on alone to deliberate his sealed play, Black 99.

For the first time that day there was cheerful conversation. 'We ran out of tobacco once when I was a boy,' said the Master, having a leisurely smoke. 'Of course everyone smoked pipes in those days. We even used to stuff our pipes with lint. It did well enough, in its way.'

A suggestion of a cool breeze had come up. Now that the Master had withdrawn from the board, Otaké, continuing his deliberations, slipped off his cloak of gossamer net.

Back in his room, the Master startled us again by challenging Onoda to Shōgi. After Shōgi, it is said, there was mahjong.

The site of combat having become unbearably oppressive, I fled to the Fukujuro Inn at Tōnosawa. When I had finished a day's instalment of my report, I left for my summer house in Karuizawa.

27

The Master was like a starved urchin in his appetite for games. Shut up in his room with his games, he was doing his heart ailment no good. An introspective person, however, not given to easy switches of mood, he probably found that only games quieted his nerves and turned his mind from Go. He never went for walks.

Most professional Go players like other games as well, but the Master's addiction was rather special. He could not play an easy, nonchalant match, letting well enough alone. There was no end to his patience and endurance. He played day and night, his obsession somewhat disquieting. It was less as if he were playing to dispel gloom or beguile tedium than as if he were giving himself up to the fangs of gaming devils. He gave himself to mahjong and billiards just as he gave himself to Go. If one put aside the inconvenience he caused his adversaries, it might have been said, perhaps, that the Master himself was forever true and clean. Unlike an ordinary person with pre-occupations of some intensity, the Master seemed to be lost in vast distances.

Even in the interval between a session and dinner, he would be at one game or another. Iwamoto would not yet have finished his flagon of saké when the Master would come impatiently for him.

At the end of the first Hakoné session, Otaké asked the maid for a Go board as soon as he was back in his room. We could hear stones clicking as, apparently, he reviewed the course of the game. The Master, now in a cotton kimono, promptly appeared at the managers' office. With great dispatch he defeated me at five and six matches of Ninuki Renju.

'But it's such a lightweight game,' he said fretfully as he went out. 'We'll play Shōgi. There's a board in Mr Uragami's room.'

His match with Iwamoto at rook's handicap[26] was interrupted by dinner.

Happy from his evening drink, Iwamoto sat grandly with his legs crossed and slapped away at his bare thighs; and in due order he lost.

After dinner a clicking of stones came sporadically from

Otaké's room; but soon he came down for rook-handicap games with Sunada of the *Nichinichi* and myself.

'When I play Shōgi I have to sing. Excuse me, please. I do like Shōgi. I ask myself and ask myself, and for the life of me I can't understand why I became a Go player instead of a Shōgi player. I've been at Shōgi longer than Go. Must have learned it when I was four, maybe not quite, and a person ought to be stronger at the game he learned first.' He would sing happily away at his own versions, dotted with puns and innuendoes, of children's songs and popular songs.

'I imagine you're the strongest Shōgi player in the Association,' said the Master.

'I wonder. You're rather good yourself, you know, sir. But no one in the Association has made even the First Rank at Shōgi. I imagine I'll always get first play when I play Renju with you. I don't even know the standard moves. I just elbow my way ahead. I believe that you are Third Rank, sir?'

'But I doubt if I could beat even a First Rank professional. Professionalism gives a person strength.'

'The Master of Shōgi, Mr Kimura – how is he at Go?'

'Possibly First Rank. They say he's improved lately.'

Otaké hummed happily as he did battle with the Master at a no-handicap game. The Master was seduced into humming with him. Such levity was not usual with the Master. His rook having been promoted,[27] he had a slight edge.

In those days the Master's Shōgi games were cheerful and lively, but as illness overtook him that ghostlike quality became apparent. Even after the 10 August session he had to have games to divert him. To me it was as if he were suffering the torments of hell.

The next session was scheduled for 14 August. But the Master was far weaker and in great pain. The managers urged suspending the match. The newspaper had resigned itself to the inevitable. The Master made a single play on 14 August and a recess was called.

Seated at the board, each player first took his bowl of stones from the board and set it at his knee. The bowl seemed too heavy for the Master. The players in turn, following the earlier course of the match, laid the stones out as at the end of the last session. The Master's stones seemed about to slip through his fingers, but as the ranks took shape he seemed to gain strength, and the click of the stones was sharper.

Absolutely motionless, the Master meditated for thirty-three minutes over his one play. It had been agreed that White 100 would be sealed.

'I can play a little more, I think,' said the Master.

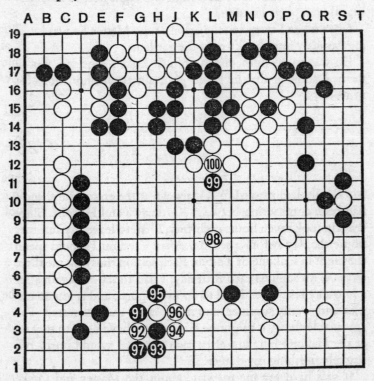

Figure 7: Ninth and Tenth Sessions (Moves 91–100)

No doubt he was in a mood for battle. The managers h
a hasty conference. But a promise was a promise. It was
decided to end the session with the one sealed play.

'Very well, then.' Even after he had sealed his White 100,
the Master gazed on at the board.

'It has been a long time, sir, and I have caused you a great
deal of trouble,' said Otaké. 'Do care for yourself.'

'Yes,' was all the Master said. His wife answered at greater
length.

'Exactly a hundred plays. How many sessions?' Otaké asked
the recorder. 'Ten? Two in Tokyo and eight here in Hakoné?
Exactly ten plays a session.'

Later when I went to take leave of the Master he was looking vacantly into the sky over the garden.

He was to go immediately into St Luke's Hospital, but it
seemed unlikely that he could get train accommodations for
some days.

28

My family had moved to Karuizawa at the end of July, and I
had been commuting between Karuizawa and Hakoné. Since
the trip took seven hours each way, I had to leave my summer
house the day before a session. After a session I would spend
the night in Hakoné or Tokyo. Each session thus cost me three
days. With sessions each fifth day, I had to set out again after
a two-day rest. Then I had to do my reports, and it was an un-
pleasantly rainy summer, and in the end I was exhausted. The
reasonable thing, it might be said, would have been to stay on
at the Hakoné inn; but after each session I would hurry off,
scarcely finishing my dinner.

It was hard for me to write about the Master and Otaké
when we were together at the inn. Even when I stayed over-

night at Hakoné I would go down to Miyanoshita or Tōno-sawa. It made me uncomfortable to write about them and then be with them at the next session. Since I was reporting on a match sponsored by a newspaper, I had to arouse interest. A certain amount of embroidering was necessary. There was little chance that my amateur audience would understand the more delicate niceties of Go, and for sixty or seventy instalments[28] I had to make the manner and appearance and gestures and general behaviour of the players my chief material. I was not so much observing the play as observing the players. They were the monarchs, and the managers and reporters were their subjects. To report on Go as if it were a pursuit of supreme dignity and importance – and I could not pretend to understand it perfectly – I had to respect and admire the players. I was presently able to feel not only interest in the match but a sense of Go as an art, and that was because I reduced myself to nothing as I gazed at the Master.

I was in a deeply pensive mood when, on the day the match was finally recessed, I boarded a train at Ueno Station for Karuizawa. As I put my baggage on the rack, a tall foreigner hurried over from across the aisle some five or six seats forward.

'That will be a Go board.'

'How clever of you to know.'

'I have one myself. A great invention.'

The board was a magnet decorated with gold leaf, very convenient for playing on a train. In its cover it was not easy to recognize as a Go board. I was in the habit of taking it with me on my travels, since it added little to my baggage.

'Suppose we have a game. I am fascinated with it.' He spoke in Japanese. He promptly set the board on his knees. Since his legs were long and his knees high, it was more sensible to have the board on his knees than on mine.

'I am Thirteenth Class,'[29] he said with careful precision, as if doing a sum. He was an American.

I first tried giving him a six-stone handicap. He had taken lessons at the Go Association, he said, and challenged some famous players. He had the forms down well enough, but he had a way of playing thoughtlessly, without really putting himself into the game. Losing did not seem to bother him in the least. He went happily through game after game, as if to say that it was silly to take a mere game seriously. He lined his forces up after patterns he had been taught, and his opening plays were excellent; but he had no will to fight. If I pushed him back a little or made a surprise move, he quietly collapsed. It was as if I were throwing a large but badly balanced opponent in a wrestling match. Indeed this quickness to lose left me wondering uncomfortably if I might not have something innately evil concealed within me. Quite aside from matters of skill, I sensed no response, no resistance. There was no muscular tone in his play. One always found a competitive urge in a Japanese, however inept he might be at the game. One never encountered a stance as uncertain as this. The spirit of Go was missing. I thought it all very strange, and I was conscious of being confronted with utter foreignness.

We played on for more than four hours, from Ueno to near Karuizawa. He was cheerfully indestructible, not in the least upset however many times he lost, and seemed likely to have the better of me because of this very indifference. In the face of such honest fecklessness, I thought myself rather perverse and cruel.

Their curiosity aroused by the novel sight of a foreigner at the Go board, four or five other passengers gathered around us. They made me nervous, but they did not seem to bother the foreigner who was losing so effortlessly.

For him it was probably like having an argument in a foreign language learned from grammar texts. One did not of course wish to take a game too seriously, and yet it was quite clear that playing Go with a foreigner was very different from playing Go with a Japanese. I wondered whether the point might be that foreigners were not meant for Go. It had more than once been remarked at Hakoné that there were five thousand devotees of the game in Dr Dueball's Germany, and that it was beginning to attract notice in America too. One is of course rash to generalize from the single example of an American beginner, but perhaps the conclusion might be valid all the same that Western Go is wanting in spirit. The Oriental game has gone beyond game and test of strength and become a way of art. It has about it a certain Oriental mystery and nobility. The 'Honimbō' of Honimbō Shūsai is the name of a cell at the Jakkōji Temple in Kyoto, and Shūsai the Master had himself taken holy orders. On the three-hundredth anniversary of the death of the first Honimbō, Sansa,[30] whose clerical name was Nikkai, he had taken the clerical name Nichion. I thought, as I played Go with the American, that there was no tradition of Go in his country.

Go came to Japan from China. Real Go, however, developed in Japan. The art of Go in China, now and three hundred years ago, does not bear comparison with that in Japan. Go was elevated and deepened by the Japanese. Unlike so many other civilized arts brought from China, which developed gloriously in China itself, Go flowered only in Japan. The flowering of course came in recent centuries, when Go was under the protection of the Edo Shogunate. Since the game was first imported into Japan a thousand years ago, there were long centuries when its wisdom went uncultivated. The Japanese opened the reserves of that wisdom, the 'road of the three hundred and sixty and one',[31] which the Chinese had seen to encompass the principles of nature and the universe and of human life, which they had named the diversion of the immortals, a game of abundant spiritual powers. It is clear that in Go the Japanese spirit has transcended the merely imported and derivative.

Perhaps no other nation has developed games as intellectual as Go and Oriental chess. Perhaps nowhere else in the world would a match be allotted eighty hours extended over three months. Had Go, like the Nō drama and the tea ceremony, sunk deeper and deeper into the recesses of a strange Japanese tradition?

Shūsai the Master told us at Hakoné of his travels in China. His remarks had to do chiefly with whom he had played and where and at what handicap.

'So I suppose the best players in China would be good amateurs in Japan?' I asked, thinking that Chinese Go must after all be fairly strong.

'Something of the sort, I should think. They may be a touch weaker, but I should think a strong amateur there would be a match for a strong amateur here. They have no professionals, of course.'

'If their amateurs and ours are about equal, then you might say that they have the makings of professionals?'

'I think you might.'

'They have the potential.'

'But it won't happen overnight. They do have some good players, though, and I gather that they like to play for stakes.'

'They have the material.'

'They must, when they can produce someone like Wu.'

I meant to visit Wu of the Sixth Rank soon. As the retirement match took shape, much of my interest turned to the shape his commentary was taking. I thought of it as a sort of aid and supplement to my report.

That this extraordinary man was born in China and lived in Japan seemed symbolic of a preternatural bounty. His genius had taken life after his remove to Japan. There had been numerous examples over the centuries of persons distinguished in one art or another in a neighbouring country and honoured in Japan. Wu is an outstanding modern example. It was Japan that nurtured, protected, and ministered to a genius that would have lain dormant in China. The boy had in fact been discovered by a Japanese Go player who lived in China for a time. Wu had already studied Japanese writings on Go. It seemed to me that the Chinese Go tradition, older than the Japanese, had sent forth a sudden burst of light in this boy. Behind him a profound source of light lay buried in the mud. Had he not been blessed with a chance to polish his talents from his very early years, they would have lain forever hidden. No doubt in Japan too, remarkable Go players have remained in obscurity. Such is the way of the fates with human endowments, in the individual and in the race. Examples must be legion of wisdom and knowledge that shone forth in the past and faded towards the present, that have been obscured through all the ages and into the present but will shine forth in the future.

29

Wu of the Sixth Rank was in a sanitarium at Fujimi, to the west of Mt Fuji. After each of the Hakoné sessions, Sunada of the *Nichinichi* would go to Fujimi for his comments. I would insert them appropriately into my report. The *Nichinichi* had chosen him because he and Otaké were the reliables among younger players, strong competitors in skill and in popularity.

He had over-exerted himself at Go and fallen ill. And the war with China grieved him deeply. He had once described in an essay how he longed for an early peace and the day when Chinese and Japanese men of taste might go boating together on beautiful Lake T'ai. During his illness at Fujimi he studied such works as *The Book of History*, *Mirror of the Immortals*, and *Collected Works of Lu Tsu*.[32] He had become a naturalized Japanese citizen, taking Kuré Izumi as his Japanese name.

Although the schools were out when I returned from Hakoné to Karuizawa, that international summer resort was crowded with students. There was gunfire. Troops of student reserves were in training. More than a score of acquaintances in the literary world had gone off with the army and navy to observe the attack on Hankow. I was not selected for the party. Left behind, I wrote in my *Nichinichi* reports of how popular Go had always been in time of war, of how frequently one heard stories of games in battle encampments, of how closely the Way of the Warrior resembled a way of art, there being an element of the religious in both.

Sunada came to Karuizawa on 18 August and we took a train on the Kōmi line from Komoro. One of the passengers reported that in the heights around Mt Yatsugataké great numbers of centipede-like insects came out in the night to cool themselves, in such numbers that the train wheels spun as if the tracks had been greased. We spent the night at the Saginoyu hot spring in Kamisuwa and went on the next morning to Fujimi.

Wu's room was above the entrance. In one corner were two tatami mats. He illustrated his remarks with small stones on a small wooden board which he had laid out upon a small cushion and a collapsible wooden stand.

It was in 1932 at the Dankōen in Itō that Naoki Sanjūgo and I watched Wu play the Master at a two-stone handicap. Those six years before, in a short-sleeved kimono of dark blue speckled with white, his fingers long and slender, the skin fresh at the nape of his neck, he had made one think of an elegant and sensitive young girl. Now he had taken on the manner of the cultivated young monk. The shape of the head and ears and indeed of every feature suggested aristocracy, and few men can have given more clearly an impression of genius.

His comments came freely, though occasionally he would stop, chin in hand, and think for a time. The chestnut leaves glistened in the rain. How in general would he characterize the game, I asked.

'A very delicate game. It is going to be very close.'

It had been recessed in its early middle stages, and the Master himself was a contestant; and it was not for a rival player to predict the outcome. Yet what I wanted were comments upon the manner of play, given a sense of mood and style – an appraisal of the game as a work of art.

'It is splendid,' he replied. 'In a word, it is an important game for both of them, and they both are playing carefully. They are giving a great deal of thought to every move. I can't see a single mistake or oversight on the part of either. You aren't often treated to such a game. I think it's splendid.'

'Oh?' I was somewhat dissatisfied. 'Even I can see that Black is playing a tight game. Is White too?'

'Yes, the Master is playing very carefully, very tightly. When one side plays a tight game the other must too, or he will find his positions crumbling. They have plenty of time, and it's a very important game.'

It was a bland, harmless appraisal, and the appraisal I had hoped for was not forthcoming. Perhaps it had been bold of him even to describe the game as a close one.

But since I was in a state of great excitement over a game I had studied intently through all its early phases, I had hoped for something more profound, something touching on the spiritual.

Saitō Ryūtarō of the magazine *Bungei Shunjū* was convalescing at a near-by inn. We stopped to see him. He had until recently been in the room next to Wu's.

'Sometimes in the middle of the night when everyone else was asleep I would hear stones clicking. It was a little hairraising, actually.' And he remarked upon the extraordinary dignity with which Wu saw visitors to the door.

Shortly after the Master's retirement match, I was invited with Wu to Shimogamo Springs in South Izu, and I learned about dreams of Go. Sometimes, I was told, a player discovers a brilliant play in his sleep. Sometimes he remembers a part of the configuration after he awakens.

'I often have a feeling when I'm at the board that I have seen a game before, and I wonder if it might have been in a dream.'

His most frequent adversary in dreams, said Wu, was Otaké of the Seventh Rank.

30

'The game has to be recessed,' I have heard that the Master said before he went into St Luke's, 'but I don't want outsiders looking at an unfinished game and saying that White is doing well and Black is doing all right too.'

It was the sort of thing the Master would have said; but there are probably shifts in the tides of battle that are quite impossible for an outsider to understand.

Apparently the Master was optimistic. Once after the match was over he remarked to Goi of the *Nichinichi* and myself: 'When I went into the hospital I didn't think White was in at all a bad position. I did think some odd things were happening, but I was not really worried.'

Black 99 'peeped at'[33] a White open connection, and with White 100, the last play before he was hospitalized, the Master joined his stones. Afterwards, in his review of the game, he said that if he had not so joined his stones but rather sought to control the Black formation to the right of the board and prevent an incursion into White territory, 'the outlook would not have been such as to permit sanguineness on Black's part'. He seems to have been satisfied with the early course of the game. The fact that he had been able to play White 48 on a 'star point' and so to 'control the passes' in the opening stages 'meant what anyone must concede to be an ideal White formation'. It followed, he said, that 'Black 47, giving up the strategic point, was too conservative a play', which could not 'evade charges of a certain tepidness'.

Otaké, however, in his own reflections, said that if he had not played as he did there would still have been openings for White in the vicinity, and these he was loath to permit. Wu's commentary agreed with Otaké's. Black 47 was the proper play, he said, and left Black with massive thickness.

I can remember gasping when Otaké closed his lines at Black 47 and White took the strategic star point with White 48. It was less that I felt Otaké's style of play in Black 47 than that I felt the formidable resolve with which he had entered the match. He sent White back to the third line and plunged in to build his own massive wall; and I felt absolute commitment. He had taken his position. He was not going to lose the game and he was not going to be deceived by White's subtle stratagems.

If at White 100, in the middle phase of the game, the outcome seemed uncertain, then Black was being outplayed by White; but the point may have been that Otaké was playing a strong but careful game. Black had the greater thickness and Black territory was secure, and the time was at hand for Otaké's own characteristic turn to the offensive, for the gnawing into enemy formations at which he was so adept.

Otaké of the Seventh Rank has been called a reincarnation of Honimbō Jōwa.[34] Jōwa was the great master of the aggressive game. Honimbō Shūsai too has been likened to Jōwa. The essence of Jōwa's game was to build strong walls, move forward into open battle, and throw everything into a frontal assault. It was a grand and turbulent style of Go, even a gaudy style, replete with crises and rich in shifts and variations, very popular among amateur fanciers of the game. The amateur audience for this the Master's final game therefore expected power against power, violent clash upon violent clash, until the board had become one glorious entanglement. That expectation could scarcely have been betrayed more thoroughly.

Otaké seemed cautious of challenging the Master at his own game. His initial object to limit the Master's freedom of motion and avoid difficult entanglements over a broad front, he set about shaping his ranks after patterns he had made peculiarly his own. Allowing the Master a strategic point, he was all the while buttressing his own walls. What may at first sight have seemed passive was in fact a strong undercurrent of aggression and an unshakable confidence. What may have seemed mere tenacity had a surging power. True to his own uncompromising aims he would from time to time launch forth violently upon the offensive.

Yet however careful Otaké might be about keeping his ranks in order, there should somewhere along the way have been a chance for the Master to lay down a serious challenge. The Master initially staked out broad claims in two of the corners. In the upper left corner, where Otaké had responded to White 18 with Black 19 at 'three-three', C-17, this the last match for the sixty-four-year-old Master was following the newer pattern; and from that corner a storm presently blew up. There if anywhere would have been the spot for the Master, had he chosen, to be difficult. But perhaps because the match was so important to him, he seemed to prefer the cleaner, less involved sort of game. Down into these middle phases the Master replied to Otaké's overtures; and as he moved ahead with what had certain elements of the one-man performance about it, Otaké found himself drawn into a close, delicate contest.

Such a match was probably inevitable, granted Black's play, and so boldness gave way to a concern for every possible point – which development might in the final analysis be taken as a success for White. The Master was not pursuing a brilliant plan of his own, nor was he taking advantage of bad play. It perhaps told of his age and experience, the fact that like the flow of water or the drifting of clouds a White formation quietly took shape over the lower reaches of the board in response to careful and steady pressure from Black; and so the game became a close one. The Master's powers had not waned with age, nor had illness damaged them.

31

'I left on 8 July, eighty whole days ago,' said Shūsai the Master, back in his Setagaya house upon his release from St Luke's. 'I've been away all through the summer and on into the fall.'

He strolled a few blocks that day, his longest venture forth in two months. His legs were weak from the months in bed. Two weeks after he left the hospital he was able, with considerable effort, to sit on his heels in the formal manner.

'I've been trained to the proper way for fifty years now. Actually I've found it easier to sit on my heels than to sit cross-legged. But after all that time in bed I couldn't manage any more. At meals I would cross my legs under the tablecloth. No, it wasn't really that I sat cross-legged. I'd throw these skinny legs of mine out in front of me. I'd never done that before in my life. I'll have to get used to long bouts of sitting on my heels or I won't be able to go on with the game. I've been working on it as best I can, but I have to admit I still have trouble.'

The season had come for horse racing, of which he was so fond. He had to be careful of his heart, but finally he could contain himself no longer.

'I thought up a good excuse. I said I had to give my legs a trial, and went out to the Fuchū track. Somehow I'm happier when I'm at the races. I felt better about my game. But I was exhausted when I got home. I suppose the core isn't very solid any more. I went again and could see no reason at all why I shouldn't be playing. I decided today that we could begin on the eighteenth.'

These remarks were taken down for publication by Kuro-saki, a reporter for the *Nichinichi*. The 'today' was 9 November. Play would thus be resumed some three months after the last Hakoné session, 14 August. Since winter was approaching, the Dankōen in Itō was chosen as the new game site.

The Master and his wife, escorted by a disciple, Murashima of the Fifth Rank, and by Yawata, secretary of the Go Association, arrived at the Dankōen on 15 November, three days in advance of play. Otaké of the Seventh Rank arrived on 16 November.

The tangerine groves were beautiful in the hills, and down at the coast the bitter oranges were turning gold. It was cloudy and chilly on the fifteenth, and on the sixteenth there was a light rain. The radio reported snow here and there over the country. But the seventeenth was one of those warm late-autumn Izu days when the air is sweet and soft. The Master walked to the Otonashi Shrine and Jōnoiké Pond. The expedition was unusual. The Master had never been fond of walking.

On the evening before the first Hakoné session he had called a barber to the inn, and at the Dankōen too, on the seventeenth he had himself shaved. As at Hakoné, his wife stood behind him supporting his head.

'Do you dye hair?' he asked the barber. His eyes were turned quietly on the afternoon garden.

He had his white hair dyed before leaving Tokyo. It may have seemed rather unlike the Master to dye his hair in preparation for battle, but perhaps he was bringing himself together after his collapse.

He had always clipped his hair short, and there was something amusingly incongruous about the long hair carefully parted and even dyed black. The Master's tawny skin and strong cheekbones emerged from the lather.

Though not as pale and swollen as at Hakoné, it was still not a healthy face.

I had gone to the Master's room immediately upon my arrival.

'Yes,' he said, absently as always. 'I was examined at St Luke's the day before I came. Dr Inada had his doubts. My heart still isn't right, he said, and there's a little water on the pleurae. And then the doctor here at Itō has found something in my bronchial tubes. I suppose I'm catching cold.'

'Oh?' I could think of nothing to say.

'I'm not over the first ailment and I get a second and a third. Three seems to be the grand total at the moment.'

'Please don't tell Mr Otaké, sir.' People from the Association and the *Nichinichi* were present.

'Why?' The Master was puzzled.

'He'll start being difficult again if he finds out.'

'And so we shouldn't keep secrets from him.'

'It would be better not to tell him,' agreed the Master's wife. 'You'll only put him off. It will be Hakoné all over again.'

The Master was silent.

He spoke openly of his condition to anyone who asked.

He had stopped both the tobacco and the evening drink of which he was so fond. At Hakoné he had almost never gone out, but now he forced himself to walk and to eat hearty meals. Perhaps dyeing his hair was another manifestation of his resolve.

I asked whether at the end of the match he meant to winter in Atami or Itō or return to St Luke's.

He replied, as if taking me into his confidence: 'The question is whether I last that long.'

And he said that his having come so far was probably a matter of 'vagueness'.

32

The mats in the game room were changed the night before the first Itō session. The room had the smell of new mats when we came in on the morning of the eighteenth. Kosugi of the Fourth Rank had gone to the Naraya for the famous board used during the Hakoné sessions. At their places, the Master and Otaké uncovered their bowls of stones. The black stones were coated over with summer mildew. With the help of the desk clerk and the maids they were cleaned on the spot.

It was ten thirty when White 100 was opened.

Black 99 had 'peeped at' the White open connection, and White 100 joined the threatened White pieces. The last session at Hakoné had consisted of the one sealed play.

'Even considering that I was very ill and that White 100 was my last play before going into the hospital,' said the Master in his comments upon the game, 'it was a somewhat ill-considered play. I should have ignored the peep and pressed ahead at S-8 and so secured the White territory off towards the lower right. Black had threatened, to be sure, but there was no immediate need for him to cut my line, and even if he had I would not have been in great difficulty. Had I used White 100 to protect my own ground, the outlook would not have been such as to permit sanguineness on Black's part.'

Yet White 100 was not a bad play, and one could not say that it weakened the White position. Otaké had assumed that the Master would respond to the 'peep' by linking his stones, and to us bystanders the linking seemed quite natural.

One would imagine that though White 100 was a sealed play Otaké had for three months known what it would be. Now, inevitably, Black 101 must strike into White territory towards the lower right. To us amateurs it seemed that Otaké had a natural play, a space removed on the 'S' line from Black 87. Yet he still had not played when noon came and the recess for lunch.

We were surprised to see the Master out in the garden during the recess. Plum branches and pine needles glistened in the sun, and there were white *yatsudé* flowers and yellow, daisylike silverleaf. On the camellia below Otaké's room a single blossom with crinkled petals had come out. The Master gazed at it.

At the afternoon session, a pine cast its shadow on the paper doors of the game room. A white-eye chirped outside. There were large carp in the pond. The carp at the Naraya in Hakoné had been of various hues. These were the natural grey.

Even the Master seemed bored. It was taking Otaké a very long time to play. The Master closed his eyes and might have been asleep.

'A difficult spot,' muttered Yasunaga of the Fourth Rank. He sat cross-legged with one foot drawn up on the other thigh. His eyes too were closed.

What was so difficult about it? I began to suspect that Otaké was deliberately holding back from the obvious play, the jump to S-7. The managers too were impatient. Otaké said in his comments after the match that he had debated whether to 'push' at S-8 or jump to S-7. The Master too said in his review of the game that it was difficult to judge the relative merits of the two plays. Yet I thought it most odd that Otaké should use three and a half hours for the first play after the long recess. The sun was low and the lights had been turned on when finally he made his decision. It took the Master only five minutes to play White 102 in the space over which Black had jumped. Otaké took forty-two minutes for Black 105. There were only five plays during the first Itō session. Black 105 became the sealed play.

The Master had used only ten minutes, and Otaké four

hours and fourteen minutes. In all Otaké had used twenty-one hours and twenty minutes, more than half the unprecedented forty-hour allotment.

Onoda and Iwamoto, the judges, were absent, participating in the autumn tournament.

'There is something dark about Otaké's game these days,' I had heard Iwamoto say at Hakoné.

'There are bright and dark in Go?'

'There are indeed. A game takes on its own shading. There's something very cheerless about Otaké's. Something dark. Bright and dark have nothing to do with winning and losing. I'm not saying that Otaké's game is any the worse for it.'

Otaké had a disturbingly unbalanced record. He had lost all eight of his matches at the spring tournament. Then, in the special tournament sponsored by the *Nichinichi* to choose the Master's last challenger, he had won all his matches.

I had not thought the Black game against the Master especially cheerful. There was something oppressive about it, something that seemed to push up from deep within, like a strangled cry. Concentrated power was on collision course, one looked in vain for a free and natural flow. The opening moves had been heavy and a sort of inexorable gnawing had followed.

I have also heard that there are two sorts of players, those who are forever dissatisfied with themselves and those who are forever confident. Otaké may be put in the former category, Wu in the latter.

Otaké, the dissatisfied sort, could not, in what he himself had called a close and delicate game, allow himself the luxury of easy, cavalier play – not while the outcome remained in doubt.

33

After the first Itō session there was a disagreement, so considerable that the date for the next session was uncertain.

As at Hakoné, the Master requested a modification of the rules because of his illness. Otaké refused to accede. He was more stubborn than he had been at Hakoné. Perhaps Hakoné had given him all the amendments he could tolerate.

I was in no position to write of the inside happenings and do not remember them as well as I might, but they had to do with the schedule.

Four-day recesses had been agreed upon, and the agreement had been honoured at Hakoné. The recesses were of course to recover from the strain of a session, but for the Master, sealed in at the Naraya as required by the 'canning' system, they had the perverse effect of adding to the strain. As the Master's condition became serious, there had been talk of shortening the recesses. Otaké had stubbornly rejected any such proposals. His one concession had been to move the last Hakoné session up a day. It had been limited to the Master's White 100; and although the schedule itself was on the whole maintained, the plan of having the sessions last from ten in the morning until four in the afternoon was abandoned.

Since the Master's heart condition was chronic and there was no way of knowing when it would improve, Dr Inada of St Luke's with great reluctance allowed the expedition to Itō, and asked that if at all possible the match be finished within a month. The Master's eyelids were somewhat swollen at the first session.

There was concern lest the Master fall ill again, and a wish to have him free from the pressures of competition as soon as possible; and the newspaper wanted somehow to bring to a conclusion this match so popular among its readers. Delays would be dangerous. The only solution was to shorten the recesses. But Otaké was uncompromising.

'We've been friends for a long time,' said Murashima of the Fifth Rank. 'Let me talk to him.'

Both Otaké and Murashima had come to Tokyo from the Osaka region as boys. Murashima had become a pupil of the Master's, Otaké had become apprenticed to Suzuki of the Seventh Rank; but no doubt Murashima took the optimistic view that, in view of their old friendship and their relations in the world of Go, a special plea from him would be effective. He went so far as to tell Otaké of the Master's ailments, however, and the result was to stiffen Otaké's resistance. Otaké went to the managers: so they had kept the Master's condition secret from him, and were asking him to do battle with an invalid?

Otaké was no doubt angered, and thought it a blot on the game, that Murashima, a disciple of the Master's, should have a room at the inn and be seeing the Master. When Maeda of the Sixth Rank, a disciple of the Master's and brother-in-law to Otaké, had visited Hakoné, he had avoided the Master's room and stayed at a different inn. And probably Otaké could not tolerate the thought that such matters as friendship and sympathy should be brought into a disagreement over a solemn and inviolable contract.

But what probably bothered him most was the thought of again having to challenge the aged Master; and the fact that his adversary was the Master made his position the more difficult.

The situation went from bad to worse. Otaké began to talk of forfeiting the match. As at Hakoné, Mrs Otaké came from Hiratsuka with her baby and sought to mollify him. A certain Tōgō, practitioner of the art of healing by palm massage, was called in. He was well known among Go players, Otaké having recommended him to numbers of colleagues. Otaké's admiration was not limited to Tōgō the healer: he also respected Tōgō's advice in personal matters. There was something of the religious ascetic about Tōgō. Otaké, who read the *Lotus Sutra* every morning, had a way of believing absolutely in anyone he was inclined to respect, and he was a man with a deep sense of obligation.

'He will listen to Tōgō,' said one of the managers. 'Tōgō seems to think he should go on with the game.'

Otaké said that this would be my chance to give Tōgō's healing powers a try. It was an honest and friendly suggestion. I went to Otaké's room. Tōgō felt here and there with the palms of his hands.

'There's nothing at all wrong with you,' he said promptly. 'You are delicate, but you will live a long life.' But for some moments he continued to hold his hands over my chest.

I too brought a hand to my chest, and noted with surprise that the quilted kimono over the right side was warm. He had brought his hands near but not touched me. The kimono was warm on the right side only, and chilly on the left. He explained that the warmth came from certain poisonous elements. I had been aware of nothing abnormal in the region of my lungs, and X-rays had revealed no abnormality. Yet I had from time to time sensed a certain pressure towards the right side, and so perhaps I had in fact been suffering from some slight indisposition. Even granting the effectiveness of Tōgō's methods, I was startled that the warmth should have come through the heavy quilting.

Tōgō said that Otaké's destiny was in the match, and to forfeit it would make him an object of universal derision.

The Master could only await the outcome of the negotiations. Since no one had informed him of the finer points, he was probably unaware that Otaké thought of forfeiting the match. He grew fretfully impatient as the days went by in useless succession. He drove to the Kawana Hotel for a change of scene and invited me to go with him. The next day I in turn took Otaké.

Though threatening to forfeit the game, Otaké had remained sealed up at the inn, and I was fairly sure that he would presently be coaxed into a compromise. On the twenty-third a compromise was in fact reached: there would be play every three days, and the sessions would end at four in the afternoon. The compromise came on the fifth day after the first Itō session.

When at Hakoné the four-day recess had been shortened to three, Otaké had said that he could not get enough rest in three days, and that two-and-a-half-hour sessions were too short. He could not find his pace. Now the three days were shortened to two.

34

One shoal had been traversed, and another lay ahead.

As soon as he heard of the compromise, the Master said: 'We'll begin tomorrow.'

But Otaké wanted to rest the next day and begin the day after.

Unhappy with the delay, the Master was poised to begin immediately. The matter seemed to him a simple enough one. But Otaké's feelings were complicated. Weary from the long days of altercation, he needed rest and a change of mood before he resumed play. The two men were of two quite different natures. Otaké was moreover suffering from nervous indigestion. And the baby, at the inn with Mrs Otaké, had caught cold and was running a high fever. Devoted to his family, Otaké was much concerned. He could not possibly play the next day.

But it had been very bad management to keep the Master waiting so long. The managers could not tell him, all eager for battle, that Otaké's convenience demanded waiting a day longer. His 'tomorrow' was for the managers absolute. Since there was also a difference in rank to consider, they sought to prevail upon Otaké. Already in a state of great tension, Otaké was much put out. He said he would forfeit the game.

Yawata of the Association and Goi of the *Nichinichi* sat in a small upstairs room, silent and to all appearances exhausted. They seemed on the verge of surrender. Neither was an eloquent or persuasive man. I sat with them after dinner.

The maid came for me. 'Mr Otaké says he would like to speak with you, please, Mr Uragami. He is waiting in another room.'

'With me?' I was startled. The two looked at me. The maid led me to a large room in which Otaké was waiting alone. Though there was a brazier, the room was chilly.

'I am very sorry indeed to bother you. You have been a great help over the months, but I have decided I have no recourse but to forfeit the game.' His speech was abrupt and hurried. 'I cannot go on as things are.'

'Oh?'

'And I at least wanted to apologize.'

I was only a battle reporter, scarcely a person to whom he need apologize. That I should all the same be the recipient of formal apologies seemed evidence of our esteem for each other. My position had changed. I could not let matters stand as they were.

I had been a passive observer of the disputes at Hakoné and after. They had not been my concern, and I had offered no opinion. Even now he was not asking my advice. He was informing me of his decision. Sitting with him and hearing of his tribulations, however, I felt for the first time that I should speak up, and indeed that I might possibly offer my services as mediator.

I spoke boldly. I said that as challenger in this the Master's last game he was fighting in single combat, and he was also fighting a larger battle. He was the representative of a new day. He was being carried on by the currents of history. He had been through a year-long tournament to determine who would be the Master's last challenger. Kubomatsu and Maeda had been the winners of an earlier elimination tournament among players of the Sixth Rank, and they had been joined by Suzuki, Segoé, Katō, and Otaké of the Seventh Rank in a tournament in which every player met every other. Otaké had defeated all five opponents. He had defeated two of his own teachers, Suzuki and Kubomatsu. Suzuki, it was said, would have bitter regrets for the rest of his life. In his prime he had won more games than he had lost as Black against the Master's White, and the Master had avoided the next stage, at which they would play Black and White in alternation.[35] Perhaps out of feelings for his old teacher, Otaké had wanted to let Suzuki have one last chance at the Master. Yet he had sent his teacher to defeat. And when he faced Kubomatsu, each of them with four victories, in the decisive match, he was again facing a teacher. One might therefore say that Otaké was playing for his two teachers in this contest with the Master. The young Otaké was no doubt a better representative of the active forces than were elders like Suzuki and Kubomatsu. His incomparable friend and rival, Wu of the Sixth Rank, would have been an equally appropriate representative, but Wu had five years earlier tried a radical opening against the Master and lost. And even though Wu had won a professional title, he had at the time been of the Fifth Rank, scarcely an eminence from which to face the Master at no handicap; and so the match had been of a different order from this the Master's last match. Some twelve or thirteen years before, and some years too before his match with Wu, the Master had been challenged by Karigané of the Seventh Rank. The contest was really between

the Go Association and the rival Kiseisha, and, though Karigané was among the Master's rivals, he had over the years been
the underdog. The Master won another victory, and that was
all. And now 'the invincible Master' was staking his title for
the last time. The match had a far different import from those
with Karigané and Wu. It was not likely that problems of
succession would arise immediately if Otaké were to win, but
the retirement match meant the end of an age and the bridge
to a new age. There would be new vitality in the world of Go.
To forfeit the match would be to interrupt the flow of history.
The responsibility was a heavy one. Was Otaké really to let
personal feelings and circumstances prevail? Otaké had thirty-
five years to go before he reached the Master's age – five more
than the sum by the Oriental count of his years thus far. He
had been reared by the Association in a day of prosperity, and
the Master's youthful tribulations were of a different world.
The Master had carried the principal burden from the begin-
nings of modern Go in early Meiji through its rise to its recent
prosperity. Was not the proper course for his successors to see
this match, the last of his long career, to a satisfactory end? At
Hakoné the Master had behaved in a somewhat arbitrary
fashion because of his illness, but still an old man had endured
pain and gone on fighting. Not yet fully recovered, he had
dyed his hair black to continue the battle here at Itō. There
could be little doubt that he was staking his very life on it. If
his young adversary were to forfeit, the sympathies of the
world would be with the Master, and Otaké must be resigned
to sharp criticism. Even if Otaké's case was a good one, he
could expect nothing better than endless affirmations and
denials, or perhaps a contest in mudslinging. He could not
expect the world to recognize the facts. This last match would
be history, and a forfeiture would be history too. The most
important point of all was that Otaké carried responsibility for
an emerging era. If the game were to end now, conjecture on

the final outcome would become a matter of noisy and ugly rumours. Was it really right for a young successor to ruin the Master's last game?

I spoke hesitantly and by fits and starts. Yet I made what were for me a remarkable number of points. Otaké remained silent. He did not agree to continue the match. He of course had his reasons, and repeated concessions had brought him to the breaking point. He had just made another concession, and been ordered as a result to play on the morrow. No one had shown the slightest concern for his feelings. He could not play well in the circumstances, and so the conscientious thing was not to play at all.

'If we postpone it a day, you will go on?'

'Yes, I suppose so. But there's no good in it, really.'

'But you will play the day after tomorrow?'

I pushed for a clear answer. I did not say that I would speak to the Master. He continued to apologize.

I returned to the managers' room. Goi lay with his head pillowed on an arm.

'He said he wouldn't play, I suppose.'

'That's what he wanted to tell me.' Yawata's broad back was haunched over the table. 'But it seems he will go on if we postpone it a day. Shall I ask the Master? Do I have your permission?'

I went to the Master's room. 'As a matter of fact, sir, I have a favour to ask. I know I'm not the one to do it, and you may think me presumptuous; but might we postpone our next session till the day after tomorrow? Mr Otaké says that one more day is all he asks. His baby is running a high fever, and he is very upset. And he is having trouble with his digestion, I believe.'

The Master listened, a vacant expression on his face. But his answer was prompt: 'That is entirely acceptable. We shall do as he wishes.'

Startled, I felt tears coming to my eyes.

The problem had been almost too easily disposed of. I found it difficult to leave immediately. I stayed for a time talking with the Master's wife. The Master himself had nothing more to say, either about the postponement or about his adversary. A day's postponement may seem like a small enough concession. The Master had waited a very long time, however, and for a player midway through a match, all poised for a session, to have his plans suddenly thrown into confusion was no small matter at all. Indeed it was of such magnitude that the managers could not bring themselves to approach the Master. He no doubt sensed that the request had taken all the resolve I had. His quiet, almost casual acquiescence touched me deeply.

I went to the managers and then to Otaké's room.

'The Master agrees to play the day after tomorrow.'

Otaké seemed surprised.

'He has conceded a point this time. Perhaps if something else comes up you can concede a point?'

Mrs Otaké, at the baby's side, thanked me most courteously. The room was in great disorder.

35

Play was resumed on the appointed day, 25 November, a full week after the preceding session. Onoda and Iwamoto, the judges, neither at the moment occupied with the autumn tournament, had come the night before.

Cushion of vermilion damask, purple armrest – the Master's place was a priestly one. And indeed the line of Honimbō, Masters of Go, had been clerics from the day of the founder, Sansa, whose clerical name was Nikkai.

Yawata of the Association explained that the Master had in fact taken orders and the priestly name Nichion and that he owned clerical robes. On a wall above the Go board was a framed inscription by Hampō: 'My Life, a Fragment of a Landscape'. Gazing up at the six Chinese characters, which leaned to the right, I remembered having read in the newspaper that this same Dr Takada Sanaé[36] was gravely ill. Hanging on another wall was an account by Mishima Ki,[37] who used the nom de plume Chūshū, of the twelve famous places of Itō. On a hanging scroll in the next room, an eight-mat room, was a poem in Chinese by a wandering mendicant monk.

A large oval brazier of paulownia was at the Master's side. Because he feared he might be coming down with a cold, he had water boiling on an oblong brazier behind him. At the urging of Otaké he wrapped himself in a muffler, and as further defence against the cold he was buried deep in a sort of over-cloak with a knitted lining. He was running a slight fever, he said.

The sealed play, Black 105, was opened. The Master took only two minutes to play White 106; and another period of deliberation began for Otaké.

'Very odd,' Otaké muttered, as if in a trance. 'I'm running out of time. The great man is running out of time, forty whole hours of it. Very odd. Nothing like it in the whole history of the game. Still wasting time there, are you? Should have played in one minute, no more.'

Incessantly, under a cloudy sky, bulbuls whistled and called. I went to the veranda and saw that an azalea by the pond was in bud and indeed had sent forth two unseasonal blooms. A grey wagtail came up to the veranda. Faint in the distance was the sound of a motor pump, bringing water from the hot spring.

Otaké took an hour and three minutes for Black 107. Black 101, invading the White formation in the lower right-hand corner, was an offensive play demanding a response and worth a potential fourteen or fifteen points, and Black 107, though it did not require an immediate response, extended Black's territory towards the lower left, and was worth some twenty points. In both cases it seemed likely to us observers that considerable profit would redound to Black, and in both cases Black was favoured by the order of the moves.

Now the offensive had passed to White. A stern, intent expression on his face, the Master closed his eyes and breathed deeply. In the course of the session his face had taken on a coppery flush. His cheeks twitched. He seemed to hear neither the wind nor the drum[38] of a passing pilgrim. Yet he took forty-seven minutes for his next play. It was his one prolonged period of deliberation during the Itō sessions. Otaké took two hours and forty-three minutes for Black 109, which became

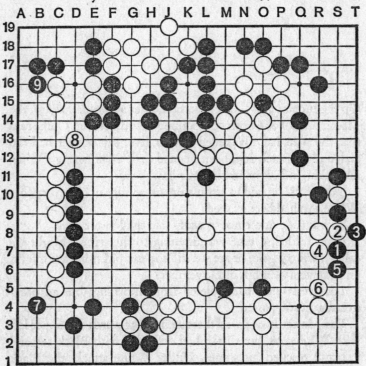

Figure 8: First and Second Itō Sessions (Moves 101–109)

the sealed play. The match had advanced only four plays. Otaké had used three hours and forty-six minutes, the Master but forty-nine minutes.

'Anything could happen now,' said Otaké, half jesting, as he left for the noon recess. 'It's murderous.'

White 108 had the double aim of threatening Black in the upper left-hand corner and cutting away at Black's inner fast-nesses, and of defending the White formation at the left of the board. It was a happy device.

Wu said of it in his commentary: 'White 108 was an extremely difficult play. One waited with not a little excite-ment to see where it would fall.'

36

On the morning of the next session, after a two-day recess, the Master and Otaké both complained of indigestion. Otaké said that the pain had awakened him at five. No sooner had the sealed play, Black 109, been opened than Otaké excused him-self, taking off his overskirt as he left.

'Already?' he said in astonishment, seeing on his return that White 110 had been played.

'It was rude of me not to wait,' said the Master.

Arms folded, Otaké was listening to the wind. 'Might we call it a wintry gale, or are we still too early? I think we might, on the twenty-eighth of November.'

The west wind had quieted from morning, but an occa-sional gust still passed.

The Master had glared threateningly towards the upper left with White 108, but Otaké had defended with Black 109 and 111 and rescued his stones. Under White attack, the Black ranks in the corner faced difficulties. Would the Black stones die, would the *kō* situation[39] arise? The possibilities were as varied as in a textbook problem.

'I must do something about that corner,' said Otaké as Black 109 was opened. 'It's on long-term loan, and the interest is high.' And he proceeded to solve the riddle the corner had presented and to restore calm.

Today, surprisingly, the match had advanced five plays by eleven in the morning. Black 115 was not an easy play for Otaké, however. The time had come to stake everything on a grand assault.

Waiting for Black to play, the Master talked of eel restaurants in Atami, the Jūbako and the Sawashō and the like. And he told of having come to Atami in the days before the railway went beyond Yokohama. The rest of the journey was by sedan chair, with an overnight stop in Odawara.

'I was thirteen or so, I suppose. Fifty and more years ago.'

'Ages and ages ago,' smiled Otaké. 'My father would just about then have been born.' Complaining of stomach cramps, he left the board two or three times while deliberating his next move.

'He does take his time,' said the Master during one of the absences. 'More than an hour already?'

'It will soon be an hour and a half,' said the girl who kept the records. The noonday siren blew. 'Exactly a minute,' she said, looking at the stopwatch of which she was so proud. 'It begins to taper off at fifty-five seconds.'

Back at the board, Otaké rubbed Salomethyl on his forehead and pulled at the joints of his fingers. He kept an eye medicine called Smile beside him. He had not seemed prepared to play before the noon recess, but at eight minutes after the hour there came the smart click of stone on board.

The Master grunted. He had been leaning on an armrest. Now he brought himself upright, his jaw drawn in, his eyes rolled upwards as if to bore a hole through the board. He had thick eyelids, and the deep lines from the eyelashes to the eyes set off the intentness of his gaze.

White now needed to defend his inner territories against the clear threat presented by Black 115. The noon recess came.

Otaké sat down at the board after lunch and immediately went back to his room for a throat medicine. A strong odour spread through the room. He put drops in his eyes and two hand-warmers in his sleeves.

White 116 took twenty-two minutes. The plays down to White 120 came in quick succession. The standard pattern would have had the Master falling quickly back with White 120, but he chose a firm block even though the result was an unstable triangular formation. The air was tense, for a showdown was at hand. If he had given ground it would have been to concede a point or two, and he could not make even so small a concession in so tight a match. He took just one minute for a play that could mean the fine difference between victory and defeat, and for Otaké it was like cold steel. And was the Master not already counting his points? He was counting with quick little jerks of his head. The count pressed on relentlessly.

Games can be won and lost by a single point. If White was clinging stubbornly to a mere two points, then it was for Black to step boldly forward. Otaké squirmed. For the first time a blue vein stood out on the round, childlike face. The sound of his fan was rough, irritable.

Even the Master, so sensitive to the cold, was nervously fanning himself. I could not look at the two of them. Finally the Master let out his breath and slipped into an easier posture.

'I start thinking and there's no end to it,' said Otaké, whose play it was. 'I'm warm. You must forgive me.' And he took off his cloak. Prompted by Otaké, the Master pulled back the neck of his kimono with both hands and thrust his head forward. There was something a little comical about the act.

'It's hot, it's hot. Here I am taking forever again. I wish I didn't have to.' Otaké seemed to be fighting back a reckless impulse. 'I have a feeling I'm going to make a mistake. Make a botch of the whole thing.'

After meditating on the problem for an hour and forty-four minutes, he sealed his Black 121 at three forty-three in the afternoon.

For the twenty-one plays during the three Itō sessions, Black 101 to Black 121, Otaké had used eleven hours and forty-eight minutes. The Master had used only one hour and thirty-seven minutes. Had it been an ordinary match, Otaké would have exhausted his time allotment on a mere eleven plays.

One could see in the divergence a spiritual incompatibility,

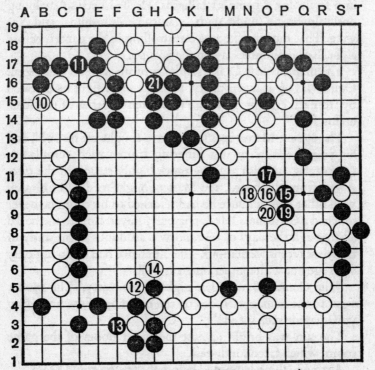

Figure 9: Third Itō Session (Moves 110–121)

and perhaps something physiological as well. The Master too was known as a careful, deliberate player.

37

Every night the west wind blew; but the morning of the next session, 1 December, was warm and pleasant. One looked for springlike shimmerings in the air.

After a game of Shōgi the day before, the Master had gone into town for a game of billiards. He had been at mahjong until almost midnight with Iwamoto, Murashima, and Yawata. That morning he was out strolling in the garden before eight. Red dragonflies lay on the ground.

The maple below Otaké's upstairs room was still half green. Otaké was up at seven-thirty. He feared he might be defeated by stomach cramps, he said. He had ten varieties of medicine on his desk.

The ageing Master seemed to have fought off his cold, and his young adversary was suffering from varied complaints. Otaké was, surprisingly, the more highly strung of the two. Away from the board, the Master sought to distract himself with other games. Once he had returned to his room he never touched a Go stone. Otaké apparently stayed close to the board all through the days of rest and was assiduous in his study of the most recent formations. The difference had to do not only with age but with temperament as well.

'The Condor flew in last night at ten thirty.' The Master went to the managers' room on the morning of the first. 'Can you imagine such speed!'

The sun was bright against the paper doors of the game room, which faced south-east.

A strange thing happened before the session could begin.

Having submitted the seals for verification, Yawata opened the envelope. He leaned over the board, the chart in his hand, and looked for Black 121. He could not find it.

The player whose turn it is at the end of a session marks his sealed play on the chart, which he puts in an envelope, showing it to no one. At the end of the preceding session Otaké had stepped into the hall to set down his play. The two players had put their seals on the envelope, which Yawata had sealed in a larger envelope, kept in the safe of the inn through the recess. Thus neither the Master nor Yawata knew Otaké's play. The possibilities were limited, however, and the play seemed fairly predictable to us who were watching. We looked on in great excitement. Black 121 might well be the climax of the game.

Yawata should have found it immediately, but his eyes wandered over the chart.

'Ah!' he said at length.

I was some slight distance from the board, and even after the Black stone had been played I had difficulty finding it. When presently I did find it, I was at a loss for an explanation. Off in the remote upper reaches of the board, it lay apart from the fight that was coming to a climax at the centre.

Even to an amateur like myself it had the look of a play from the *kō* situation to a distant part of the board.[40] A wave of revulsion came over me. Had Otaké taken advantage of the fact that Black 121 was a sealed play? Had he put the device of the sealed play to tactical use? If so, he was not being worthy of himself.

'I expected it to be near the centre,' said Yawata, smiling wryly as he drew back from the board.

Black had set out to destroy the massive White position from the lower right towards the centre of the board, and it seemed quite irrational that at the very height of the attack he should play elsewhere. Understandably, Yawata had looked for the sealed play in the battle zone, from the centre down towards the right. The Master shielded his 'eyes'[41] by playing

White 122 in response to Black 121. If he had not, the eight White stones at the top of the board could have been killed. It would have been as if he had declined to answer a play from *kō*.

Otaké reached for a stone, and went on thinking for a time. His hands tightly folded on his knees, his head cocked to one side, the Master sat in an attitude of great concentration.

Black 123, which took three minutes, brought Otaké back to the task of cutting into the White formation. He first invaded the lower right corner. Black 127 turned once more to the centre of the board, and Black 129 finally lashed out to decapitate the triangle the Master had so stubbornly put together with White 120.

Wu of the Sixth Rank commented: 'Firmly blocked by White 120, Black embarked with resolution upon the aggressive sequence from Black 123 to Black 129. It is the sort of play, suggesting a strongly competitive spirit, which one sees in close games.'

But the Master pulled away from this slashing attack, and, counter-attacking to the right, blocked the thrust from the Black position. I was startled. It was a wholly unexpected play. I felt a tensing of my muscles, as if the diabolic side of the Master had suddenly been revealed. Detecting a flaw in the plans suggested by Black 129, so much in Otaké's own characteristic style, had the Master dodged away and turned to in-fighting by way of counter-attack? Or was he asking for a slash so that he might slash back, wounding himself to down his adversary? I even saw in that White 130 something that spoke less of a will to fight than of angry disdain.

'A fine thing,' Otaké muttered over and over again. 'A very fine thing.' He was still deliberating Black 131 when the noon recess was called. 'A fine thing he's done to me. A terrible thing, that's what it is. Earthshaking. I make a stupid play myself, and here I am with my arm twisted behind me.'

'This is what war must be like,' said Iwamoto gravely.

He meant of course that in actual battle the unforeseeable occurs and fates are sealed in an instant. Such were the implications of White 130. All the plans and studies of the players, all the predictions of us amateurs and of the professionals as well had been sent flying.

An amateur, I did not immediately see that White 130 assured the defeat of 'the invincible Master'.

38

Yet I was aware that something unusual had happened. Whether we somehow followed the Master to lunch or whether he somehow invited us to come with him I do not know, but we were in his room; and as we sat down he said in a low but intense voice: 'The match is over. Mr Otaké ruined it with that sealed play. It was like smearing ink over the picture we had painted. The minute I saw it I felt like forfeiting the match. Like telling them it was the last straw. I really thought I should forfeit. But I hesitated, and that was that.'

I do not remember whether Yawata was with us, or Goi, or both. In any case, we were silent.

'He makes a play like that, and why?' growled the Master. 'Because he means to use two days to think things over. It's dishonest.'

We said nothing. We could neither nod assent nor seek to defend Otaké. But our sympathies were with the Master.

I had not been aware, at the moment of play, that the Master was so angry and so disappointed as to consider forfeiting the match. There was no sign of emotion on his face or in his manner as he sat at the board. No one among us sensed his distress.

We had been watching Yawata, of course, as he was having

his troubles with the chart and the sealed play, and we had not looked at the Master. Yet the Master had played White 122 in literally no time, less than a minute. It was understandable that we should not have noticed. The minute had not started precisely when Yawata found the sealed play, to be sure; and yet the Master had brought himself under control in a very short time, and maintained his composure throughout the session.

To have these angry words from the Master, who had so nonchalantly made his next play, was something of a shock. I felt in them a concentrated essence, the Master doing battle from June down into December.

The Master had put the match together as a work of art. It was as if the work, likened to a painting, were smeared black at the moment of highest tension. That play of black upon white, white upon black, has the intent and takes the forms of creative art. It has in it a flow of the spirit and a harmony as of music. Everything is lost when suddenly a false note is struck, or one party in a duet suddenly launches forth on an eccentric flight of his own. A masterpiece of a game can be ruined by insensitivity to the feelings of an adversary. That Black 121 having been a source of wonder and surprise and doubt and suspicion for us all, its effect in cutting the flow and harmony of the game cannot be denied.

Black 121 was much discussed among the professionals of the Go world and in the larger world as well. To an amateur like me the play most definitely seemed strange and unnatural, and not at all pleasing. But afterwards there were professionals who came forward and said that it was time for just such a play.

'I had been thinking that the time was ripe for Black 121 one of these times,' said Otaké in his 'Thoughts after Combat'.

Wu touched only lightly on the play. After a diagonal and connection on White's part at E-19 and F-19, he said, 'White need not respond as the Master did with 122 even to Black's

121, but could defend himself at H-19. Black would thus find the possible *kō* threats more limited.'

No doubt Otaké's explanation would have been similar.

Black 121 had come as the battle at the centre was reaching a climax, and it had been a sealed play. It had angered the Master and aroused suspicions in the rest of us. In a difficult situation, a player might, in effect, make a sealed play like Black 121 as a temporary expedient, and until the next session, in this case three days later, give thought to what the last play of the preceding session should in fact have been. I had even heard of players who, at perhaps one of the grand tournaments, would play as if from *kō* to the far reaches of the board while the last allotted seconds were being read off, and so prolong life a few seconds more. All manner of devices had been invented to make use of recesses and sealed plays. New rules bring new tactics. It was not perhaps entirely accidental that each of the four sessions since play had been resumed at Itō had been ended with a sealed play on the Black side.

The Master was so ready for a showdown that he said afterwards: 'The time had passed for pulling back with White 120.' And the next play was this Black 121.

The important point, in any case, is that Black 121 angered and disappointed the Master that morning.

In his review of the game the Master did not touch upon Black 121.

A year later, however, in 'Selected Pieces on Go', from *Collected Works of the Master*, he spoke out quite openly. 'Now was the time to make effective use of Black 121 . . . We must note that if he proceeded at his leisure (which is to say waited until White had played the diagonal followed by the connection), there was a chance that Black 121 would not suffice.'

Since Otaké's opponent himself made the admission, little doubt should remain. He was angry at the time because the move was so unexpected. In his anger he unjustly questioned Otaké's motives.

Perhaps, embarrassed at the want of clarity, the Master made a special point of touching upon Black 121. But is it not more likely that, in a work published a year after the match and a half year before his death,[42] he remembered the proportions of the controversy and quietly recognized the play for what it was?

The Master's 'now' was Otaké's 'one of these times'. To an amateur like me something of a puzzle still remained.

39

Another puzzle: why did the Master play White 130 and so ensure his own defeat?

He made the play at eleven thirty-four, after twenty-seven minutes of deliberation. It was a matter of chance, I suppose, that he should have made a bad play after deliberating almost a half hour. Yet I was sorry afterwards that he had not waited another hour and so carried the play past the noon recess. If he had left the board and taken an hour and a half's rest, he would probably have played more effectively. He would not have fallen victim to a passing wraith, so to speak. He had twenty-three hours of play remaining, and need not have worried about an hour or two. But the Master was not one to make tactical use of a recess. It was Black 131 that had the advantage of the recess.

White 130 seemed like a counter-attack at close quarters, and Otaké said that he had been left with his arm twisted behind him.

This was Wu's comment: 'It is a delicate spot. White 130 may be seen as an effective play in response to a cutting thrust.'

Yet White should not have retreated before the thrust, however telling. To pull back from a conflict so fierce, a challenge so determined, means to give way completely.

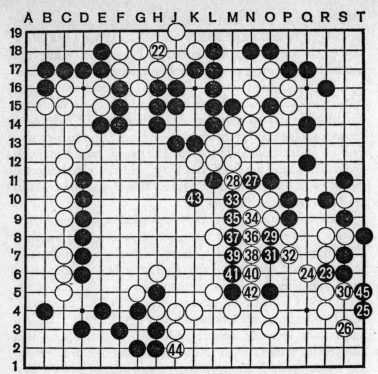

Figure 10: Fourth Itō Session (Moves 122–145)

Through the Itō sessions Otaké had played a careful, solid game, control reinforcing control, tenacity backing up tenacity. The sudden eruption of his accumulated powers came with the cut at Black 129. Otaké seems to have been by no means as startled and confused by White's withdrawal as the rest of us were. If White took the four black stones to the right, Black would quite simply overrun the White ranks towards the centre of the board. Black did not respond to White 130, but extended Black 129 with Black 131. White returned to the defence at the centre with White 132. He should rather have responded directly to Black 129.

The Master lamented the play in his review of the match.

'White 130 was the fatal error. The proper sequence would have been to cut immediately at P-11, and see how Black replied. If for instance he replied at P-12, then White 130 would be the correct play. Even if he extended, as with Black 131, White need not hurry with the oblique extension at Q-8, but could quietly consolidate his ranks with M-9. Whatever variations might have occurred, the lines would have been more complex than on the chart as we have it, and an extremely close fight would have ensued. The *coup de grâce* came with the assault following upon Black 133. However desperate he might be in his search for remedies, White was powerless to send the crushing wave back.'

The fatal play suggested a psychological or a physiological failure. I myself, amateur though I am, thought at the time that with White 130, which seemed a strong play and which seemed a quiet, withdrawn sort of play, the Master, consistently on the defensive, was trying to turn the tide; and at the same time I felt that his patience was at an end, his temper taxed to the breaking. But he said that if he had cut Black at a single point he could have saved himself. It would seem that the mistake resulted from more than an outburst of the anger the Master had felt all morning. Yet one cannot be sure. The Master himself could not have measured the tides of destiny within him, or the mischief from those passing wraiths.

As the Master played White 130, the sound of a virtuoso flute came drifting in, to quiet somewhat the storm on the board.

The Master listened. He seemed to be reminiscing.

> '*From high in the hills, see the valley below.*
> *Melons in blossom, all in a row.*

'The first piece you learn on the flute. There is another kind of bamboo flute, you know, with one hole less than this one. The single-joint,[43] they call it.'

Otaké pondered over Black 131 for an hour and fifteen

minutes, exclusive of the noon recess. At two in the afternoon he took up a stone.

'Shall I?' He paused and finally played.

The Master, seated bolt upright, thrust his head forward and rapped irritably on the rim of the brazier. He glared at the board. He was counting up points.

The White triangle that had been cut off by Black 129 was cut on the other side by Black 133, and, with white stones in check play after play down to Black 139, the 'earthshaking' changes of which Otaké had spoken took shape around and below the three white stones. Black had invaded the very heart of the White formation. I could almost hear the sound of the collapse.

'I don't know. It's all the same. I don't know,' muttered the Master, fanning himself furiously. Should he take the two black stones beside him or pursue his line of flight? 'I don't know, I don't know.'

But he played with remarkable speed, in twenty-eight minutes. Tea and refreshments were brought in.

'I'm not feeling well, thank you.' Otaké declined the helping of *mushizushi*⁴⁴ the Master pressed upon him.

'Think of it as medicine.'

'I was sure this would be the sealed play,' said Otaké, contemplating White 140. 'You play so fast, sir, you have my head spinning. Nothing upsets me more.'

Black 145 was the sealed play. Otaké took a stone in his hand and went on thinking, and the time appointed for the end of the session arrived. He withdrew into the hall to set down his sealed play. The Master continued to gaze at the board. His lower eyelids seemed inflamed and somewhat swollen. Through the sessions at Itō he was constantly looking at his watch.

40

'I think I would like if possible to finish today,' the Master said to the managers on the morning of 4 December. In the course of the morning's session he said to Otaké: 'Suppose we finish today.' Otaké nodded quietly.

The faithful battle reporter, I felt a tightening in my chest at the thought that after more than half a year the match was to finish today. And the Master's defeat was clear to everyone.

It was also in the morning, at a time when Otaké was away from the board, that the Master turned to us and smiled pleasantly. 'It's all over. Nothing more to be done.'

I do not know when he had called a barber, but this morning he resembled a shaven-headed priest. He had come to Itō with his hair long and parted, as in the hospital, and dyed black; and now, suddenly, it was cropped short. One might have seen histrionics in this refashioning; yet he seemed young and brisk, as if a layer of ageing had been washed away.

4 December was a Sunday. There were one or two plum blossoms in the garden. Since numbers of guests had come to the inn on Saturday, the session was held in the new addition, in the room that had always been mine, next to the Master's. The Master's room was at the far end of the new building. The managers had the night before occupied the two rooms directly above. They were in effect protecting the Master from incursions by other guests. Otaké, who had been on the second floor of the new building, had moved downstairs a day or two before. He was not feeling at all well, he said, and it was a trial to climb up and down stairs.

The new building faced directly south. The garden was wide and open, and direct sunlight fell near the Go board.

His head inclined to one side, his brows wrinkled and his torso sternly upright, the Master gazed at the board while Black 145 was being opened. Otaké played more rapidly, perhaps because he knew he had won.

The tension of the final encounter at close quarters is unlike that through the opening and middle stages. Raw nerves seem to flash, there is something grand and even awesome about the two figures pressing forward into closer combat. Breath came more rapidly, as if two warriors were parrying with dirks; fires of knowledge and wisdom seemed to blaze up.

It was the time when, in an ordinary game, Otaké would be going into his sprint, playing a hundred stones in the course of his last allotted minutes. He still had a margin of some six or seven hours, and yet, as if riding the wave of his aroused nerves he seemed intent upon keeping his momentum. He would reach for a stone as if whipping himself on, and then, from time to time, he would fall into deliberation. Even the Master would sometimes hesitate when he had a stone in his hand.

Watching these last stages was like watching the quick motions of a precisely tooled machine, a relentless mathematical progression, and there was an aesthetic pleasure too in the order and the formal propriety. We were watching a battle, but it took clean forms. The figures of the players themselves, their eyes never leaving the board, added to the formal appropriateness.

From about Black 177 to White 180, Otaké seemed in a state of rapture, in the grip of thoughts too powerful to contain. The round, full face had the completeness and harmony of a Buddha head. It was an indescribably marvellous face – perhaps he had entered a realm of artistic exaltation. He seemed to have forgotten his digestive troubles.

Perhaps too worried to come nearer, Mrs Otaké, that splendid Momotarō of a baby in her arms, had been walking in the garden, from which she gazed uneasily towards the game room.

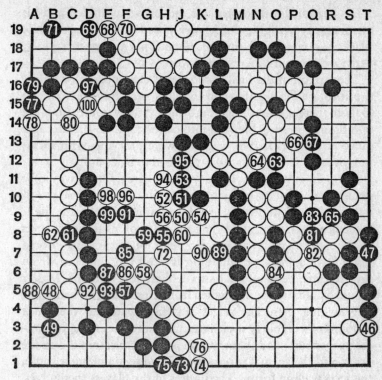

Figure 11: Start of the Final Session (Moves 145–200)

The Master, who had just played White 186, looked up as the long siren sounded from the direction of the beach. 'There's room for you all,' he said amiably, turning towards us.

The autumn tournament having ended, Onoda of the Sixth Rank was in attendance. Others too were watching as the battle pressed to a close: Yawata of the Association, Goi and Sunada of the *Nichinichi*, the Itō correspondent for the *Nichinichi*, the managers and other functionaries. They were crowded together just inside the anteroom, and some were beyond the partition. The Master was inviting them to watch from nearer the board.

That Buddha countenance lasted for but a moment. Otaké's face was alive again with a lust for battle. The small, beautifully erect figure of the Master as he counted up points seemed to take on a grandeur that stilled the air around him. When Otaké played Black 191, the Master's head fell forward, his eyes were wide, he moved nearer the board. Both men were fanning themselves violently. The noon recess came with Black 195.

The afternoon session was moved back to the usual site, Room 6 in the main building. The sky clouded over from shortly after noon, and crows cawed incessantly. There was a light above the board, a sixty-watt bulb. The glare from a hundred watts would have been too much. Faint images the colour of the stones fell across the board. Perhaps in special observance of this last session, the innkeeper had changed the hangings in the alcove for twin landscapes by Kawabata Gyokushō.[45] Below them was a small statue of a Buddha on an elephant, and beside that a bowl of carrots, cucumbers, tomatoes, mushrooms, trefoil parsley, and the like.

The last stages of a grand match, I had heard, were so horrible that one could scarcely bear to watch. Yet the Master seemed quite unperturbed. One would not have guessed that he was the loser. A flush came over his cheeks from about the two hundredth play, and he seemed a trifle pressed as for the first time he took off his muffler; but his posture remained impeccable. He was utterly quiet when Otaké made the last play, Black 237.

As the Master filled in a neutral point, Onoda said: 'It will be five points?'

'Yes, five points,' said the Master. Looking up through swollen eyelids, he made no motion towards rearranging the board. The game had ended at forty-two minutes past two in the afternoon.

'I judged before they had redone the board[46] that it would be five points,' said the Master, smiling, when the next day he

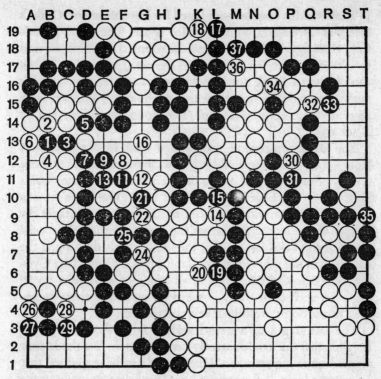

Figure 12: Close of the Final Session (Moves 201–237). White 210 at the point of 203; Black 223 at F–10

had given his thoughts on the game. 'I judged it would be sixty-eight against seventy-three. But I think if you actually redid the board you would not find that many.' He rearranged the board for himself, and came to a score of fifty-six for Black against fifty-one for White.

Until Black succeeded in destroying the White formation after that fatal White 130, no one had predicted a five-point difference. It had been careless of the Master not to take the offensive and cut at P–11 with perhaps White 160, the Master himself said, for he lost a chance thereby to reduce the proportions of Otaké's victory. One can see that such a play would have narrowed the difference to perhaps three points, even with that unfortunate White 130. What would have been the outcome, then, if the Master had not blundered and the 'earthshaking' changes had not come? A defeat for Black? An amateur like myself cannot really say, but I do not think that Black would have lost. I had come almost to believe as an article of faith, from the manner, the resolve, with which Otaké approached the game, that he would avert defeat even if in the process he must chew the stones to bits.

But one may say too that the sixty-four-year-old Master, gravely ill, played well to beat off violent assaults from the foremost representative of the new regulars until the moment late in the game when the initiative quite slipped from his hands. Neither was he taking advantage of poor play by Black nor was he unfolding a grand strategy of his own. The natural flow led into a close and delicate match. Yet perhaps because of his health the Master's game lacked persistence and tenacity.

'The Invincible Master' had lost his final match.

'The Master seems to have made it a principle to put everything into a game with the next in line, the one who might succeed him,' said a disciple.

Whether or not the Master himself had so stated the principle, he acted upon it throughout his career.

The next day I went home to Kamakura. Then, scarcely able to finish my sixty-six newspaper instalments, I went as if fleeing the battlefield on a trip to Isé and Kyoto.

I have heard that the Master stayed on at Itō, and gained weight, some four pounds, until he weighed upwards of seventy pounds; and that he visited a military convalescent home with twenty sets of Go stones. By the end of 1938, hot-spring inns were being used as convalescent homes.

41

It was New Year of the second year afterwards, just upwards of a year after the end of the retirement match: the Master and two of his disciples, Maeda of the Sixth Rank and Murashima of the Fifth Rank, attended New Year observances at the school (he offered lessons in his Kamakura house) of the Master's brother-in-law, Takahashi of the Fourth Rank. The day was 7 January. I saw the Master for the first time since the match.

He played two practice matches, but they seemed to tire him. No sound seemed to emerge from the stones as he dropped them lightly, unable to keep them between his fingers. During the second match his shoulders heaved occasionally from his breathing. His eyelids were swollen. The swelling was not particularly noticeable, but I thought of how he had been at Hakoné. He was still unwell.

Since his opponents were amateurs and the matches were for practice, the Master should have had no trouble winning. As always, however, he quite lost himself in play. We had dinner reservations at a seaside hotel and the second match was suspended at Black 130. The Master's opponent was a strong amateur of the First Rank, whom he gave a four-stone handicap. Black showed strength from the middle stages of the game and was pushing into White's broad but rather thin positions.

'Black seems to have the better of it?' I asked Takahashi.

'Yes,' he said. 'It's a blackish board. Black is thicker. White is having trouble. Our Master is getting a little senile. He breaks more easily than he used to. He can't really play any more, as a matter of fact. He's gone down at a fearful rate since that last match.'

'Yes, he does seem to have taken on the years in a hurry.'

'He's turned into a sweet old gentleman. I doubt if it would have happened if he had won that last game.'

'I will see you in Atami,' I said to the Master as I left the hotel.

The Master and his wife arrived at the Urokoya on 15 January. I had been staying at the Juraku from some days earlier. My wife and I went to the Urokoya on the afternoon of the sixteenth. The Master immediately brought out a Shōgi board, and we played two games. I am an inept Shōgi player and was not enthusiastic, and he had no trouble defeating me even at a rook-bishop handicap.[47] He urged repeatedly that we stay for dinner and a good talk.

'It's really too cold,' I said. 'When it's warmer we must go to the Jūbako or the Chikuyō.' There had been flurries of snow that day.

The Master was fond of eels.

After we left he had a hot bath, I was told. His wife had to help him. Later, in bed, he was taken with chest pains and had trouble breathing. He died before dawn two days later. Takahashi informed us by telephone. I opened the shutters. The sun was not yet up. I wondered if that last visit had been too much of a strain.

'And he was so eager to have us for dinner,' said my wife.

'Yes.'

'And she kept urging us too. I thought it was wrong of you to refuse. She had told the maid that we would be with them for dinner.'

'I knew that. But I was afraid he might catch cold.'

'I wonder if he understood. He did want us to stay, and I wonder if he wasn't hurt. He didn't at all want us to go. We should have quietly accepted. Don't you suppose he was lonely?'

'Yes. But he was always lonely.'

'It was cold, and he saw us to the door.

'Stop. I don't like it. I don't like having people die.'

The body was taken back to Tokyo that day. It was carried from the hotel in a quilt, so tiny that it scarcely seemed to be there at all. My wife and I stood a short distance off, waiting for the hearse to leave.

'There are no flowers,' I said. 'Go find a florist. Quick, before it leaves.'

My wife ran off for flowers, and I gave them to the Master's wife, who was in the hearse with the Master.

Notes

Notes

1. Shōgi, which shares a common Indian ancestor with the Western game of chess, is played on eighty-one squares with twenty pieces per side. Most pieces can be 'promoted', which is to say that they acquire greater freedom of motion upon penetrating deep into enemy territory. Captured pieces may be put back into play by the capturing side.
2. The counting of instalments is not consistent throughout the narrative. The number sixty-four would seem to include sixty-two instalments in the narrative proper plus a sort of entr'acte following the suspension of the Hakoné sessions and an epilogue at the end of the match.
3. A complex process of consolidating and simplifying the lines takes place at the end of an important match, to make the outcome clear to the most untutored eye.
4. The 'throwing of beans' to drive out malign influences. The rites occur during the first week in February, midway between the winter solstice and the vernal equinox. There is a touch of fiction here, for the sign of the zodiac under which Mr Kawabata was in fact born fell in 1935 and not again until 1947.
5. The rest of the chapter combines, with some revision, the larger portions of two of Mr Kawabata's newspaper articles.
6. *Nozoki*, a sort of tentative challenge.
7. Though the rules are complex, the basic object of Renju is to line up five Go stones in a row.
8. The expression *hoshi*, or 'star point', refers to any one of the nine points marked on the board for handicap stones (of which there are none in this title match). Here it would indicate one of the corner stars, each four lines in from either side. An opening play on a star is bold and innovative. The *komoku*, or 'little point', the most conservative point for an opening play, is three lines and four lines in from any corner. See the diagram on page 33.

9. Wu Ch'ing-yüan, born in Fukien Province in 1917. He is far more famous under the Japanese version of his name, Go Sei-gen; but he will be called Wu throughout this translation. The game of Go and Goi the newspaper reporter seem to introduce quite enough possibilities for confusion without Go the player of Go.

10. This is the storm so vividly described by Tanizaki in the second book of *The Makioka Sisters*.

11. The match, in point of fact, took place in 1933.

12. He did 'jump', playing at S-7, the second point from that occupied by his own Black 87 (see diagram, page 73). To 'push' would have been to play at S-8, adjacent to Black 87.

13. A version of Renju (see note 7) in which stones may be captured.

14. From a schoolchildren's song.

15. *Bōshi*, 'cap', two points in from an enemy position. Here (see diagram, page 71) White 50.

16. *Tsuki-atari*, 'dead end'. White 52.

17. In actual fact the seventh session was held on 31 July, and the eighth on 5 August.

18. The 'lance' (Japanese *kōsha*, 'fragrant chariot') moves forward, and forward only, any number of spaces, and so corresponds to no piece in the Western game. At a one-lance handicap, the stronger begins with one lance to his opponent's two.

19. Respectively: Confucian and historian, 1780–1832; statesman, 1836–88; and critic, essayist, and student of Chinese, 1823–1909.

20. There are special celebrations upon entering the eighty-eighth year by the Oriental count, or on the eighty-eighth birthday by the Western.

21. A variety of Renju in which, after a limited number of stones have been used on one part of the board, play must jump to another part.

22. The puzzle requires an intricate rearrangement of rectangles in a very limited space.

23. See note 13.

24. The gold general and the silver general (*kinshō* and *ginshō*) are the king's bodyguards in Shōgi. Normally silver may, upon penetrating deep into enemy territory, be promoted to gold; but under certain circumstances the advantages are in having it remain silver.

25. 'Korean Shōgi' is played with pawns alone. Pieces are lost when caught between enemy pieces.
26. There is only one rook per side even in a no-handicap game of Shōgi.
27. Upon 'promotion' it may move one space diagonally, in addition to the moves permitted the Western rook.
28. See note 2.
29. *Kyū*, 'Classes', precede *Dan*, 'Ranks', and, unlike the latter, rise in descending numerical order. The foreigner thus has thirteen steps to go before he reaches the First Rank.
30. 1558–1623.
31. Nineteen squared, the number of points on the Go board.
32. All Chinese. The first is a Confucian classic, the others are neo-Taoist.
33. See note 6.
34. The twelfth Honimbō, 1787–1847.
35. Which is to say, on completely equal terms. In no-handicap matches, Black is held to have the advantage. It will be apparent that 'the invincible Master' has in fact been defeated, though only in practice matches.
36. A president of Waseda University, member of the Diet, and Minister of Education; 1860–1938. 'Hampō' is a nom de plume or 'elegant sobriquet'.
37. Student of Chinese, 1830–1919.
38. The *hokkedaiko* or 'lotus drum' of the Nichiren (Lotus) Sect.
39. *Kō* (Sanskrit *kalpa*) is a Buddhist term for an enormous passage of time, the next thing to eternity. In Go it refers to a situation in which the two players could take and retake the same stones for all eternity without affecting the larger disposition of forces. To cut the exchange short, the player whose stone is first taken must play elsewhere on the board before returning to the scene.
40. Though the *kō* situation is not present, Black has withdrawn from the scene of action as he would be required to were it present.
41. Vacant points within a group needed to keep the group of stones from being captured.
42. In actual fact, the Master died just over a year after the end of the match.

43. *Hitoyogiri*, 'single section of bamboo'. The couplet is from a children's song.
44. Rice mixed with vegetables and, commonly, the meat of crustaceans.
45. 1842–1913.
46. See note 3.
47. There are only one bishop and one rook per side in Shōgi.